I0582598

BECOMING SOLO

A BRIGHT STAR WITCHES NOVELLA

JOYCE REYNOLDS-WARD

Copyright © 2022 by Joyce Reynolds-Ward

Cover image © 2014, downloaded from Pixabay using BookBrush. Designed in BookBrush by Joyce Reynolds-Ward

A version of *Becoming Solo* was previously released on Vella.

All rights reserved.

This is a work of fiction. All characters and events portrayed in this book are fictitious, and any resemblance to real people is purely coincidental.

No generative AI has been used in the conceptualization, development, or drafting of this work.

NO PERMISSION IS GIVEN FOR THE USE OF THIS MATERIAL FOR AI TRAINING PURPOSES.

All rights reserved.

No part of this book may be reproduced in any form or by any electronic or mechanical means, including information storage and retrieval systems, without written permission from the author, except for the use of brief quotations in a book review.

100% HUMAN CREATED.

❀ Formatted with Vellum

CHAPTER 1

A WITCH ALWAYS PROTECTS THEIR MAGIC FAIR

T*he witch who wins the Fair Crown is responsible for nurturing the Fair daemon against all outside magical influence, until they sing the Tapestry for the following year's Fair.*

The Witches Guide, Sixth Edition

"WHO'S THAT?" KIRSTEN STOPPED SUDDENLY FROM HER BACKWARDS walk, but not soon enough to keep the heavy wooden panel they were carrying as part of the Bright Star Magic Fair setup from ramming into Yesenia's gut.

She yelped. "Hey! Watch out!" She nearly dropped her end of the panel.

Mother of Magic, no!

Yesenia kept the end from hitting the ground. The contact would erase the preprogrammed magic that would activate once the panel was joined with its kin.

Once Yesenia was certain of her grip, she glared at the blonde at the other end.

1

"Kirsten, damn it, you're going to screw up my hands if you do this again!"

"Doesn't the Witches Guide always say that your voice is more important than your hands at the Fair?" Kirsten kept her voice light, but concern tightened her face. "I'm sorry, Yeni."

"Another whack like that in the gut will muck up my Tapestry Sing. Then where will we be?" Yesenia frowned at Kirsten. "And voice alone doesn't get the setup done."

"I *know*. I'm sorry, but—" Kirsten jerked her head at something behind Yesenia. "See who Rosalee's talking to. Just *look*."

Yesenia turned her head. She gasped and fumbled her end of the panel. It slipped from her fingers and fell to the ground, but she paid no attention.

Rosalee Hinds, the Style Revue and sewing spell competition superintendent for the Bright Star Magic Fair, was talking to a lanky stranger.

A stranger.

In the Style Revue setup tent, where Rosalee was the only non-magical Typical person allowed to be present. Definitely *no* outside witches were permitted inside the Fair during setup, so what was going on?

The Bright Star Fair daemon under Yesenia's custody stirred irritably as Yesenia felt the hot, pulsating, iron of the *other's* alien magic. It strained against the confines placed on it by Yesenia's personal daemon. It had willingly submitted to those restraints when Yesenia had won the Fair Crown last year, giving her the right to be the Tapestry Singer this year.

However, now it was just *so close* to the new Tapestry's birth. That made the Fair daemon, normally compliant the rest of the year, irritable and reactive to any sort of outside magic.

"Who's that witch?" Kirsten continued. "She's *strong*. I feel the power radiating off of her. My daemon recognizes her but it can't give me her name. What about yours?"

Yesenia raised her hand. "*Quiet*, Kay." She evoked *Command* in her voice, using the power given to her by the custody of the Bright Star Fair daemon to silence her friend.

Bad enough that Bright Star stirred prematurely, during setup, but *that stranger's* presence disturbed both it and her personal daemon! She had to settle them before their mutual agitation roiled the daemons belonging to the other witches in the tent. Then there would be havoc and the Fair might fail of its purpose—

She switched her attention from *that stranger* and concentrated on her daemon.

Copper. Copper, she thought to it, feeding her daemon more power to keep Bright Star restrained. *Copper, not iron,* she projected to the Fair daemon.

The Bright Star daemon stirred sullenly. *Iron burns.*

Yesenia exhaled. *Iron will not touch you or your child.* She visualized copper-shaded arms wrapping around the gravid, snakelike daemon, refocusing the daemon on the Tapestry it brooded. *Have faith. Iron will not touch you or your child.*

The Bright Star Fair daemon curled around the swelling partway down its length, but its golden eyes flickered, alert, prepared to guard its offspring. It rested its head on its coils and its eyes remained open.

Not a good thing, not at all. A bad omen that the Fair daemon stirred before setup was finished, for both the Fair and for Yesenia. She had to do something, and *soon*, before magic twisted backwards.

"What's going on?" Tobias shouted from the band stage, an anxious tone in his deep bass voice, stroking his gray-streaked brown beard nervously. "Who's using magic?"

"We have an outsider present!" Yesenia yelled. "Everyone. Shelter your daemons. The Fair daemon stirs but is resting. I will take care of it."

She left Kirsten to hold the panel upright as she marched toward Rosalee. Even though Rosalee wasn't a witch, she had been around enough witches and magic to know better! Was she trying to sabotage the Fair or what?

At least Rosalee's intricately carved, protection-spell-laden cane glowed in blues and greens. It spoke of proximity to a powerful young magician, but didn't burn in the bright orange warning of an immediate threat.

But this was still a witch that Kirsten's daemon knew. From where?

This magician wasn't forgettable, for certain. Her dark brown skin shimmered with authoritative protection spells gyring over it. Black braids vibrated with the aura of a heated iron bar. One small but muscular hand moved with an economical grace to emphasize what she was saying to Rosalee, while the other held the hanger of a long dress bag that dangled over her shoulder, the glow of a magical containment radiating off of it.

Oh, that magic tasted familiar, *so* familiar. Yesenia also recognized it as she approached Rosalee and the stranger.

So why couldn't she remember the stranger's name? She focused harder on the woman, not wanting to disturb her personal daemon's focus on soothing the restless Fair daemon.

That bag. *That bag.* It brought back memories. A style intended to restrain the powerful mix of magic and fabric that made up a Fair competition dress. A bag with a very distinctive pattern both of magic and design—where *had* she seen *that* particular bag before?

As Yesenia approached Rosalee and the strange magician, she finally remembered.

State Fair last year. She had lost Best in Style to this witch.

So what was her name?

Yesenia couldn't remember. And that was a problem.

I should remember. She kept me from being able to go Solo after State Fair.

"Rosalee." She kept her voice calm, not letting her own upset show. "Why is there a strange witch in the Fair setup?"

"Oh!" The older woman startled. "I didn't think setup was that far along."

Yesenia scowled, glaring not at Rosalee but the stranger.

This witch should know better. *Rosalee* should know better. The stranger's abilities must have befuddled Rosalee's usual awareness.

"I'm sorry," the strange witch said. "I thought I had dampened my daemon sufficiently—"

"Well, you haven't!" Yesenia snapped. "It's leaking out and making my Fair's daemon unhappy! Do you want to create a Lost Fair?"

The other witch's face grayed in shock. "No, no, no." She extended her hands toward Yesenia, palms facing her. "No ill intent meant, Fair Crown." She started backing toward the door. "I'm sorry."

Rosalee shook her head. Her eyes widened and her mouth formed an O, before she started talking rapidly. "Oh my God. Yesenia. I don't know what came over me. I honestly didn't think—oh dear, how badly are things fouled up? Are we at risk of losing the Fair?"

"Everyone is keeping control of their daemons, and the Fair daemon has settled." Yesenia made her voice steady and calm, not just for Rosalee's sake, but for the Bright Star daemon. "But for the Mother of Magic's sake, *don't do it again.*"

Rosalee bowed to Yesenia. "I will make sure that it does not happen again, Fair Crown." She frowned. "But we still need to speak with her." She jerked her head toward the open tent flap, where the strange witch had retreated, past the wards.

The wards that hadn't flared in warning, like they should have.

"After setup," Yesenia said, pondering this concern.

"After setup, in the Fair office," Rosalee echoed.

"I will see you then."

Rosalee bowed again, then left.

Yesenia knelt beside the door to check the wards.

No sign of tampering or interference.

Now *that* was a real problem.

She renewed the wards, checked the Fair daemon, whose eyelids now drooped as it returned into brooding lassitude, and turned back to the other magicians in the tent, who had all halted work to watch her speak to Rosalee and the strange witch.

Why didn't I feel them stop?

"Well?" she challenged. "Let's get back to work! We have a Fair to prepare."

The Bright Star Fair daemon crooned softly in its sleep as the aura of magical workings resumed. As it should be.

Yesenia shook her head.

Things weren't right. She heaved a heavy sigh as she rejoined Kirsten.

"Well?" the blonde challenged. "Who is she?"

"I still don't know her name," Yesenia said. "But she beat me in Style at State Fair last year."

"Ohhh. *Her.*" Kirsten frowned "She stole that title from you, Yeni."

"That's not what the judges said." Yesenia tightened her lips.

Kirsten tossed her head. "That's what *I* think. So what is *she* doing here?"

"I don't know. I just wanted to get her out of here before all the daemons—including the Fair daemon—roused and started causing problems."

Kirsten paled. "It was getting that bad?"

Yesenia nodded. "But it's fixed now. And I'm talking to *her* and Rosalee once we finish setup. Which means—" she sighed again and picked up her end of the panel that Kirsten had been steadying. "We'd better take this one to the spell dump."

She pivoted around Kirsten to head for the spell dump. Her turn to walk backward.

Yesenia took the time to survey the other workers as they walked. Tobias supervised the construction of the lower-level band stage. Six other Advanced witches competing in the Clothing division carried panels, both to the band stage and the

Tapestry Stage, which would also double as the location for Style Revue, the fashion presentation displaying clothing that blended fashion and magic. Other divisions of the Fair might win Crown in some years, but—at least in Yesenia's opinion—Style was the pinnacle of applied magic.

At least it was the easiest means toward becoming Solo, a magic practitioner who didn't need to be part of a spell matrix to keep their magic after they turned twenty-one.

Don't think about that now, Yesenia chided herself. She turned her head as Maria—late for setup, *again*—and Sam carried a panel past them.

"Stage's done," Maria called as they went by. "This is the last band panel. Then we build the runway."

Yesenia glanced at the pile of panels. There would be leftovers, but not so many that the Fair Committee would criticize her wastefulness. Good. The Fair Crown doing setup the year Yesenia won her first Crown had created too few enchanted panels to accommodate the Tapestry, the band, and the runway, which deprived several Senior exhibitors from displaying their full creations.

Last year, Yesenia had enchanted far too many panels in reaction to the previous year, and been chided for it. This year—barring any major accidents that would ground the panel spells prematurely—they would have only a few extras.

The power of planning.

Yesenia, Tobias, and Kirsten had calculated the panel layout and needs long before Fair. She had reviewed procedures with her crew, so that they didn't have panels grounded before it was time.

Planning. If she had any superpower beyond her magic, that was it.

Alas, while her planning skills made Yesenia stand out from other, more impulsive witches—it was merely mundane amongst the non-magical. Not something that would earn her special notice should she have to renounce her magic.

Yesenia glanced back, then angled toward the shimmering red spell dump bubble next to the pile of panels. Enchanted panels that were either grounded or excess went inside the dump, to have their spells removed. It was a protection to keep loose, unmoderated magic from escaping Fair Crown's control, interfering with the Tapestry Sing, or bothering the Typicals who attended to gawk at the witches and buy their wares.

The spell dump was important enough to have its own, aged daemon who slept until wakened for Fair, existing the rest of the year on the residue from the spells it absorbed during Fair.

Silently, she and Kirsten upended the panel so that it rested on one narrow end.

Open, Yesenia thought to the daemon within the bubble.

A slit appeared. Yesenia and Kirsten carefully guided the panel inside, holding it steady until the daemon took hold of it.

My regards to you, she told the daemon politely.

The daemon traced along the slit with one skinny, glowing finger, to close it. A blue and yellow line followed its finger, the glow fading back to the red of the spell dump bubble to signify a good closure.

Regards for the meal and your manners, the daemon hissed, the normally sharp, atonal edges of its thoughts blunted as it drank down the spells around the panel. *Ah. Tapestry Singer, you create the tastiest spells. A good feed. My regards.*

A wave of warm, happy daemon thoughts briefly emitted from the spell dump, enfolding Yesenia and Kirsten. They giggled as they headed for the panels to pick up another one, the glow fading when they were ten feet away.

"Well, that was a happy daemon," Kirsten said.

"A nice gift," Yesenia agreed. "But it doesn't solve the question of that witch."

Hot iron, her memory whispered. *Hot iron beat copper once. Will it do so again?*

"Your designs are better than hers," Kirsten said, as they carried their panel to the runway layout.

"She beat me at State, Kay." Yesenia waited for Kirsten to ease her end down in the protected space between the lines that marked where the runway panels belonged. Then she set hers into place. Maria and Sam followed, aligning their panels with hers.

"We'll get the last one, Fair Crown!" Sam said. He and Maria hurried to the back.

Yesenia half-smiled. Sam was a new Advanced witch this year. Not a challenger for Fair Crown, but in a couple of years, perhaps—his enthusiasm was encouraging. It boded well for the ongoing health of the Fair.

"I should know who that witch is, then, because she beat me too," Kirsten muttered, keeping her voice low so no one overheard them. "Why don't I remember who she is, Yeni? This isn't right."

"Kay, trust me. By the Mother of Spells, I'm concerned. But we can't let ourselves get too distracted by her before the Sing. I'll talk to Rosalee once we're done here."

"This is *your* Fair. *Your* turf. You're so close to going Solo. Yeni, I swear I'll Challenge her if she beats you for that last Crown."

"And she'll eat you alive, Kay. *Don't*. Please." Yesenia sighed. "I'll go into the family spell matrix if I can't go Solo. I still have that option."

"What? No. I won't let the likes of *that* outsider ruin our plans. Solo together. Set up our own boutique. I *won't* let your family's spell matrix suck you dry." Kirsten's voice rose.

"Shh! If you're not careful, you'll agitate the daemons yourself!" Yesenia snapped. "Kay, believe me, I will do my best to keep that from happening. If I can."

"If I have anything to say about it, you will." Kirsten's whisper faded as Maria and Sam placed the last panel. Donna and Larisa settled the stairs at the end.

Yesenia looked around them. Tobias and his crew had set up the drums, the keyboards, and guitar stands. She eyed the main stage. The frame intended to hold the Tapestry, once she sang it, was solid, glowing the neon green that meant the spellwork had not been activated. The same neon green shimmered around the edge of all the panels.

It was time.

"Feed the last panels to the spell dump," she ordered.

With each panel's magic given to it, the happy daemon thoughts expanded until they filled the tent.

Yesenia grinned, letting the ecstasy wash over her as she raised her hands high. She summoned *copper*, its tang flooding into her mouth, building until *copper* was all Yesenia could see and taste.

Activate, she commanded.

Neon green flashed bright red. Then it faded to royal blue, pulsing between each joint.

Yesenia began her silent inspection, starting at the band stage, followed by Kirsten and the others. She checked each panel to ensure that the linkages glowed that pulsing royal blue. She ran her hands above the instruments, to be positive that they were properly enchanted.

Then she marched up the runway stairs, stomping hard and checking every complex link. Satisfied, she moved to the runway, then the main stage.

At last, she checked the Tapestry frame.

All shimmering and pulsing in royal blue, with no fading.

A *good* Activation.

"The Style setup is complete," she announced.

Her team whooped and cheered.

"Rehearsal tomorrow afternoon at two," Yesenia continued. "The Sing begins at five. Witches, make certain of your preparation. Style will show everyone at this Fair that we are the best!"

More cheers. Then the others started to drift away.

"Want a ride home?" Kirsten asked.

Yesenia shook her head. "I have to meet with Rosalee and that stranger first."

"I can wait."

Yesenia swallowed hard. "Saul plans to pick me up after work. If I'm not here—" she let her voice trail off.

"Yeni, I can explain to your mama."

"I'd just as soon not get her and the family riled up before the end of Fair. But thanks, Kay."

"You're welcome." But as Kirsten started to leave, she leaned close. "Remember, Yeni. My family will be happy to pay for your Solo status."

Yesenia shook her head again. "Kay, I have to do it this way. Thanks—but this is how it has to happen."

She *wanted* to explain it, but Great-Aunt Eufalia's compulsion to *do it this way* was too strong.

"Good luck, then." Kirsten squeezed Yesenia's hand, then left.

Yesenia looked around the tent. An auspicious start to this year's Magic Fair, even in spite of the stranger's brief incursion.

And now, it was time for her to figure out what was going on *with that witch.*

CHAPTER 2

A WITCH WILL GIVE SANCTUARY TO THE LOST

Unless there is a legitimate, validated reason, the Fair Crown will always give Sanctuary to those witches not yet Solo whose Fairs have become Lost. Exception may be granted should the Fair Crown determine that the Lost One is a threat, usually characterized by a Challenge.

The Fair Crown's Handbook, Ninth Edition

YESENIA TIGHTENED HER LIPS AND SLOWED HER STEPS AS SHE approached the Fair Office. The Fair daemon stirred uneasily, prickly with the proximity of the other witch's power.

Did the daemon detect something she didn't?

The Bright Star Fair daemon was one of the oldest Fair daemons around. It *knew* things. It had been one of the first Magic Fairs created by an alliance of native magicians and magical settlers when Typicals and missionaries breached the wards around Oregon Territory, their goal to kill daemons and magicians alike.

Rest. You are safe, Yesenia reassured the Fair daemon. She raised *copper* to reassure the daemon.

It settled, but once again, Yesenia had the sense that it was now awake and alert, watching.

It wasn't this restless last year.

She hid her worry from the Bright Star daemon. No need to roil it up further, especially since the *stranger's* magic brushed like sandpaper against Yesenia's nerves.

She inhaled deeply. Then she stomped up the steps to the modular building that held the Fair Office, slamming her feet down harder to give a non-magical alert of her approach.

Witch's Rule.

To her pleasant surprise, the rasping sensation of the *stranger* faded. She had cloaked her magic. But was that genuine submission, or was she preparing an ambush?

Yesenia gathered her magical tools before opening the door, just in case this was an attack after all. Rumors said that other Fairs had become Lost upon the appearance of a strange witch.

Witches Guide says I must offer protection. Unless she gives me Challenge.

Damn it, why did this situation have to appear during this all-crucial, all-important year?

Maybe it wasn't a case where Sanctuary was required—and yet, why would a strange magician appear at the Fair, this late in the competition year? Especially a witch not yet bearing her Solo mark?

Sanctuary or Challenge. I must be ready.

Yesenia called up three protective spells, in preparation for the stranger's response to the three questions should she have to offer Sanctuary. Or if the stranger chose to attack. She placed her sigils on each shoulder and the last in her left hand. After some thought, she made them visible to the other witch and to Rosalee. That should be sufficient warning for Rosalee not to interfere, should she be conspiring with this witch to destroy Bright Star Fair.

Then she opened the door.

Rosalee turned from her desk, paperwork in hand. "Perfect timing, Yeni—" Her voice broke off with a tremble and her eyes widened as she took in Yesenia's magic sigils. "I—don't think— you need all *that*—" she quavered, reaching for her cane and backing away from Yesenia.

"You and *this witch* entered the tent during Setup," Yesenia said slowly and carefully, doing her best to project *threat*. The Fair daemon hissed within her, adding its own displeasure to Yesenia's. "You could have disrupted the Setup, and possibly put us at risk of becoming Lost!"

"It's not her fault." The other witch's voice was low. "I was pushing her when I shouldn't have."

Yesenia whirled to face this *other*. "Why do you come to disrupt my Fair?"

First Challenge, issued in a tone intended to irritate and provoke the other's daemon should it be looking for a fight.

Hot iron flared in the *other's* dark eyes. Power shimmered between Yesenia and the *other*, as Rosalee edged toward the door. The Bright Star daemon flared even higher, hissing, ready to strike.

Then *hot iron* winked out. Yesenia thought *copper* to the Fair daemon. It hissed disapprovingly, but settled on its coils once again. The other witch softened her shoulders and dropped her eyes, slowly, carefully, opening her fingers and exposing her palms.

"I had no intention of disrupting Bright Star Fair, Crowned One."

Yesenia relaxed slightly but still remained cautious. One Challenge down.

Two more to go.

"What's your reason for being here, witch?"

Second Challenge.

Couldn't trust *anything* until this witch responded properly to all three Challenges.

Hot iron roiled again, defensive, gathering power from the grounds that made the Fair daemon agitate again. But the witch kept her eyes down, the only possible sign of an attack showing in the way her power flared around her hands.

Then that winked out.

But the witch remained mute. Not the best answer to the Second Challenge.

However, she offered no resistance.

On to the Third Challenge.

"Answer me, witch! What's your reason for being here?"

Third Challenge. The witch *had* to answer this time, or else attack.

"I—come—in—peace." The other witch forced out her words, even as her throat flared with *hot iron*. "I—do—not—challenge you, Yesenia the Steadfast!"

Hot iron faded.

She speaks true, the Bright Star daemon acknowledged in cautious, measured tones different from its earlier anger and irritation, though it still stirred restlessly. *There is a threat from her, but she speaks true.*

So I should accept her response? Yesenia asked the Fair daemon.

Some magic theorists argued that witches shouldn't listen to their daemons, especially the quixotic Fair daemons whose loyalties changed from year to year. Yesenia had never felt that way when the Bright Star daemon spoke. Especially when it reacted in this restrained, careful manner. Bright Star was *old,* and deserved respect when it chose to speak like this. Plus she had a lot of experience with Bright Star and its reactions.

The threat is not from her, the daemon said, its voice still in that cautious, vigilant mode. *You—we—must learn more.*

Then we will, Yesenia reassured the Bright Star daemon.

"I accept your response," Yesenia said.

The other woman's shoulders softened even more. Relief crossed her face.

Rosalee hobbled away from the door. She leaned heavily on her cane as she returned to her desk. "Yesenia, this is Shawn—"

"I have no name," the other witch blurted before Rosalee could say more. "Do not use that name. It no longer belongs to me."

"That's the name on your papers," Rosalee said steadily.

"Only to those without magic." The other witch's expression shifted between shame and defiance. "To those with magic, I am Nameless and Fairless." She knelt before Yesenia. "Yesenia the Steadfast, Crown of the Bright Star Fair, I plead for Sanctuary."

First ritual plea.

"You competed at State last year. You were not Nameless and Fairless then."

The other witch swallowed hard and looked down. *Hot iron* flared briefly, but less intense than before. She stared at Yesenia's feet.

Nameless and Fairless. How could this happen?

Usually Nameless, Fairless witches had committed offenses that forbade their participation in other Fairs. But Rosalee wouldn't be so guileless as to let one such as this attempt to enter the Fair. Would she?

Bright Star? Yesenia directly asked the daemon. *Has this one committed an offense against her Fair?*

The Fair daemon stirred. *No.* But there was a sense that it was starting to suffer from agitation once again—a sign it was close to birthing the Tapestry.

The other witch raised her head. "My name is amongst the Lost," she groaned, bowing low, clutching her belly as if she had been kicked. "My Fair is gone." She doubled over, keening. Her daemon's distress momentarily broke free. The Bright Star daemon hissed, rearing up, then settled again as *hot iron* darkened into *cold iron*, the witch's personal daemon mourning along with its host.

"What do you ask of me, Lost One?"

"I am in my last year of magic," the Lost One whispered. "I

plead for Sanctuary, and the right to win a third Crown at State, so that I may become Solo."

Second plea. One more, and the ritual would become complete.

"Did you have any hand in your Fair becoming amongst the Lost?" Yesenia asked gently. The Bright Star daemon hissed approvingly at Yesenia's tone.

The other witch whimpered wordlessly, keening once again. At last she raised her head, tears rolling down her cheeks.

"The destruction was brought to us by one I trusted—wrongfully so," she murmured.

"Who was this person?"

"My boyfriend. And he dared to usurp my power, even as I Sang. That destroyed the Tapestry and—"

"Destroyed your Fair." Both Yesenia and the Fair daemon shivered. "Is he still free?"

"I—am not sure."

"Why don't you know?"

The Lost One shook her head. "He escaped, after wounding me. I am sure that I injured him as much as he did me, if not worse. I am just now recovered from what he did to me; else I would have come to you sooner, and not this close to your Tapestry's birth. I beg of you. Please. I plead for Sanctuary. I must become Solo, or else lose any protection I have against his curses."

"Joining a family spell matrix is not the option?" Though Yesenia suspected that this woman, like her, would do almost anything to avoid the depersonalized magic of a spell matrix.

"It would not be powerful enough."

Well. This witch definitely faced a worse situation than she did. Yesenia exhaled.

"Do you accept and support my position as Tapestry Singer and holder of the Bright Star Fair Crown for this year?"

A faint smile twitched the corners of the Lost One's mouth. "I swear loyalty to you as Tapestry Singer and Fair Crown for *this* year's Fair."

"*This* year's Fair?"

"I have one Fair Crown, and Style Crown from State. I need one more crown to become Solo. I swear to do my best to make your Fair stronger than ever, but as for next year—"

Yesenia sighed. The rules were strict, and this one had already sworn loyalty for this year's Fair. She couldn't just throw the woman out because she planned to compete for Fair Crown.

"I accept your oath," she said quietly. "But be aware. My need is not as dire as yours, but I, too, need one more crown to become Solo."

The other witch rose, and a quick smirk crossed her lips. "Then a true and fair competition may benefit both of us, Yesenia the Steadfast." Her expression became more solemn. "I will watch should my Fair Destroyer come here in a different guise— which he has been known to do. I know his ways."

"Thank you—if not the name on your papers, then what should we call you?"

"The Destroying One took my name from me." The other witch shivered. "Call me Shadow the Question."

"Then welcome, Shadow the Question, to the Bright Star Fair." Yesenia took Shadow's hand, and called up the Bright Star daemon as witness. She traced the sign that sealed Shadow into the Fair into her palm, and the Fair daemon breathed fire into the sigil to complete it.

I hope I don't regret this.

CHAPTER 3
A WITCH HAS
THREE CHOICES...

W hen a witch reaches their twenty-first birthday,
they have three choices:
One, to release their daemon and lose their
power.

Two, to release their daemon to a spell matrix and join with
it in the channeled expression of their power.

Three, to become Solo and ascend to all the powers, privi-
leges, and responsibilities of a Solo practitioner—provided they
meet the criteria of becoming Solo.

Failure to follow one of these paths is death for the witch
and their daemon.

The Witches Guide, Twelfth Edition

FIVE O'CLOCK. YESENIA PUT ASIDE THE LAST STYLE REVUE
application she was assessing for Rosalee as she heard someone
climbing the office trailer's steps.

Rosalee flashed her a tentative smile. "Sounds like Saul is
right on time, dear."

21

As always. Predictable.

Yesenia tamped down the flood of resentment that washed through her. Plenty of women would be happy to have a steady, reliable, hard-working, good-looking man like Saul Ramos as their fiancé.

If only it weren't an issue of Family. If only I had a choice.

Saul opened the door, smiling broadly as he spotted Yesenia. "Ready to go home, my dear?"

"Of course." Yesenia forced her smile in response as she gathered her spell bag, her purse, and her lunch bag.

"Let me take those," Saul said, rushing to her side.

She handed him everything but her spell bag. Saul was part of the Ramos family spell matrix. His family's spells wouldn't mix well with her Cruz family influence, not until they were sealed in marriage. If he took her spell bag now, either the bag would react poorly and mess up Yesenia's spells, or it would influence Saul's magic so that he couldn't work the next day.

He couldn't afford not to work.

Or so he said, whenever she asked him to come to one of her competitions.

But somehow, he was always free when Maria asked him to do something.

"A good day?" Saul asked.

"Setup went well. And you?" For some reason she didn't want to tell Saul about Shadow the Question.

"Oh, things were all right." His mouth twisted into a half-frown, half-smile as they walked out the door and down the steps. "My daemon occasionally grumbles about producing computer chip anti-hacking wards, and today was one of the more complex spell days."

He didn't add *I can hardly wait to switch to the Cruz family matrix when we marry.*

Saul's manners wouldn't allow him to say that spot out loud. But Yesenia knew, just from the way her personal daemon bristled, that *his* daemon was thinking that, and if *his* daemon was thinking that—then the notion had crossed Saul's mind, at least once. Her family crafted safety wards for individuals and industry—much less routine than computer chips.

They walked quietly across the Fair grounds to the parking lot. Saul's pickup was old, and sometimes he needed to activate his daemon to keep it from conking out in the West Side traffic. Barely legal, considering Saul had never gone Solo. But as long as he encountered a witch/former witch cop and not a Typical cop, he could usually plead necessity.

Saul opened the passenger door for Yesenia. She settled in. The pickup started smoothly and they drove in silence from the Fairgrounds west, toward Forest Grove, where the extended Cruz family lived.

At last Saul spoke. "So what happens after Fair this year?"

"State Fair," Yesenia said. "If I win Fair Crown a third time, I don't need it, but adding a State Crown will enhance my status as Solo."

Saul frowned. "Yeni, are you *sure* that's what you want to do? Becoming Solo requires a lot of work."

"I've been working toward becoming Solo since my daemon first came to me." Yesenia stared out the window and not at Saul. "I know it's a lot of work. But it's what I want to do. Want to be."

"What about me?"

Now she let her gaze turn to Saul. "What about you? You can still marry me and become part of the Cruz family matrix. Study, and we'll save the money for you to go to the Academy and earn your Solo status that way. Then we would both be Solo."

"What if I don't want to become Solo?"

"That's fine, too."

Her daemon grumbled at that statement. *We need someone who can be our equal! You—we—won't be happy if we're tied to someone who isn't Solo! Besides, neither one of them want to become Solo!*

"Yeni, that's not going to work." They halted at a streetlight and Saul rubbed his face. "Not if we want to raise a family."

"You're twenty-three. I'll be twenty-one in September. There's no rush."

A pause. Then— "That's not what your mother says. Or mine."

"Since when do our mothers decide when we have a family?" Prickles ran down Yesenia's arms.

The younger a witch has their children once they come of age, the more useful they are to a spell matrix, the *Witches Guide* said. All the authorities agreed. Later children were more likely to go Solo.

Both the Cruz and Ramos spell matrices needed powerful young witches and their children. That had been part of the calculations between their families when Saul and Yesenia had become engaged on her eighteenth birthday. The union of two spell matrices was an important matter. Sometimes even more important than the wishes of those involved.

"Yeni." Saul shook his head. "Do you really think you're capable of qualifying for Solo? What if you fail?"

"Then I fail."

"We can't lose your daemon!"

Yesenia heaved a heavy sigh as they pulled into the driveway. "Saul. I'm *not* going to fail. I wouldn't have won Fair Crown for two years in a row if I didn't have the ability to qualify for Solo."

"But you lost at State."

"*Saul.*" Was he *trying* to make her doubt herself? Set her up to fail this year?

Not words she dared say, especially this close to the Cruz spell matrix.

"Yeni." He swallowed hard. "I don't want to lose you—or your daemon—on a gamble. Your family needs a Young Leader. Your Papa—" he raised his hands.

Yes. Papa.

Things wouldn't have been so bad if her brother Carlo had stayed, hadn't renounced his daemon to become an electrician... *but Carlo gets to escape and not me. Unfair.*

24

She shook her head. "Saul. I have time. Please. Give me the space, and I'll do what I can to ensure we don't lose my daemon." She would have said more, but Mama gestured at them from the front window. "Stay for dinner?" she asked politely.

Saul's lips tightened. "Not tonight, Yesenia."

No sooner had she gathered her things and stepped out of the truck than he was backing out and roaring off.

Yesenia sighed, looking after him, her shoulders slumping.

What had seemed to be the right thing to do at eighteen to make her family happy felt very different at twenty, almost twenty-one. She turned, trudging toward the door, tensing in anticipation as Aunt Marisol peered out the window from behind Mama's shoulder.

Neither Mama nor Marisol—*especially* Marisol—would be happy that Saul had left. Would figure out that they had quarreled.

There wouldn't be much peace at home tonight. If it were just Mama she had to deal with—that would be one thing. But Marisol—

Mama eyed Yesenia suspiciously as she entered the house. "What sent Saul off like that? I was planning a big dinner, to help you recharge after Fair setup."

"He didn't say." Yesenia turned her back to Mama as she tucked her spell bag into its secured cubicle. She sealed it so that only she could withdraw it, or access any of the spells—necessary protection, especially in an expanded household with curious and exploring, almost-ready-for-their-daemon witch children, as well as half-trained witches.

"Humph. They probably fought about Yesenia's delusion that she can go Solo," Aunt Marisol sniffed.

Yesenia tensed. "You'll be displaced as Mama's second in the family matrix once I marry Saul," she reminded Marisol before turning around.

Another sniff from Marisol. "As if I *could* replace your mother."

Truth.

Aunt Marisol was a capable Second to Mama in the Cruz family matrix, but she could never become Matriarch. Marisol had remained unmarried and childless, and the rules of magical family matrices were rather strict on that front. Leaders and Matriarchs had to be married, with children.

Carlo's wife Elena would have been a possible candidate to replace Mama, until Carlo renounced his daemon and left the family matrix.

Mama turned to Marisol. "Could you please check on the children? They were dawdling when I called them in for dinner."

A third sniff from Marisol, before she wheeled and swept out of the living room, trying to project a bigger presence than she actually had. To Yesenia's relief, Mama rolled her eyes once Marisol turned her back.

Marisol must have been a real—delight—today.

That boded well for the upcoming confrontation, because when Marisol tweaked Mama the wrong way, then sniped at Yesenia like she had, Mama tended to be gentle afterward. Mama and her sister-in-law did not always see eye-to-eye.

"Little one, *did* you quarrel with Saul on the way home?"

"Yes, Mama."

"*Was* it over your dream of becoming Solo?"

Yesenia *wanted* to avoid this gentle-voiced questioning. But it was harder to get angry and storm off when Mama was being reasonable and quiet-voiced, looking at her with soft, watery, big brown eyes and a quivering chin.

She looked down at her feet. "Yes, Mama."

Mama sighed. "Oh Yesenia, Yesenia. I worry about you."

"I have the ability to become Solo." Yesenia raised her head at last, facing Mama's sad gaze.

"Ability is not the only part of becoming Solo, little one."

Sorrow tinged Mama's voice. "You could earn the Fair Crown for another year, and still be denied. And then what? There are those who would delay your choice until it is too late for you to opt into the family matrix."

You mean Marisol.

"That's why my Tapestry this year must be the best ever," Yesenia said. "Mama, I don't *need* Marisol poking at me! It's a distraction, especially the night before the Tapestry Sing."

"Marisol's methods and timing are not always the best, I agree. But she is well-intentioned, little one." Mama frowned. "There are rumors that Bright Star Fair has been targeted by those who would destroy all of us who hold daemons and practice magic."

"Why, Mama?"

Mama shrugged. "Typicals who would see all magic wrecked and gone. Those who would much rather rule without the modulating effect of witches on what they would do if they were unfettered. Are you certain you have the strength to deal with such challenges, my little one?"

"My designs are good. Kirsten and I—"

"There's more to being Solo than going out on your own with a magical business. Yes, you and Kirsten create good designs. But." Mama held up one hand as Yesenia started to sputter a comment. "Kirsten is white and you are brown. Her family is rich, and we—are not. Her father is a judge. Us? None of us hold any sort of political power."

"As if that's important!"

"Are you so idealistic and naive not to recognize these realities? Oh, Yesenia." More sorrow in Mama's voice. "Do you think you're the first one in this family who has the talent to go Solo? Who has a white friend claiming to be able to help you?"

"Kirsten's my *friend*. Our magic fits."

"And you think you're the only one to whom this has happened? Your friend can buy Solo status and become part of the ruling structure. You honestly think she would come to your defense if the Witches Council decided you weren't qualified to become Solo?"

"She—would—" Yesenia's voice faltered. *Would* Kirsten support her? She *had* offered to pay for Yesenia's certification if Yesenia didn't manage to win a third Crown, either at Bright Star or at State. And they had been planning their boutique as Solo practitioners for a long time now.

But Mama's arguments—what if Kirsten's family objected if she decided to help Yesenia?

Mama nodded. "Little one, even friendship does not always overrule Family. And Kirsten's family is quite traditional when it comes to power and magic."

"Solo status requires putting the good of witchkind above Family," Yesenia whispered.

"So they say," Mama sighed. "So they say." She glanced furtively toward the kitchen. "Marisol would say otherwise."

"And how much of what Marisol says is her envy at me getting Great-Aunt Eufalia's death-gift?"

"Shh!" Mama's eyes widened as she put a finger to her lips. She leaned in close. "Even Eufalia would warn you about being overly trustful of a rich white woman, if she were still alive."

"I know," Yesenia whispered back. "She told me to be careful before she passed on her death-gift. But Mama. Even without Kirsten—*I can do it.* I can bring honor to the Cruz family matrix as Solo."

Mama shook her head, mouth tightening. "I hope you're right, little one. Because the other part about you becoming Solo? Yes, you will bring honor to the Cruz family matrix. However, becoming Solo also means that you will need to bend over backwards to avoid favoring your family—and Saul's as well. You will have to make choices, for the good of all witchkind—and dear one. I fear what that will do to you. I would much rather see you cherished, safe in Saul's arms, and loved by your children, rather than the empty glory of becoming a high-ranking Solo."

"It's what I *want*, Mama. Being Solo has called to me for *years*."

Her mother raised her hands wide, exhaling, rolling her eyes and gazing up to the sky.

"Do you hear her?" she groaned—who was she imploring when she did this? Great-Aunt Eufalia? The Mother of Magic? Yesenia never could decide.

Then Mama dropped her hands. "So be it, my daughter. But I will oppose your choice as best as I can."

"Without undue influence?"

"Much as I dislike your choice, I will respect it. However." Another furtive look around her. "There are others who may not do so."

Yesenia nodded, recognizing the warning. She glanced toward the kitchen.

"I—I want to be alone in my room tonight, Mama, so I can contemplate the Tapestry Sing tomorrow."

"Not even the smallest plate of food?"

"Not even that."

Not safe. Marisol had been known to sneak compulsion spells into Yesenia's food in the past, and she was good enough to evade Mama's scans. While Marisol's tricks worked for managing the young, half-trained witches of the family when they were overtired and refused to listen—Marisol had never stopped trying to influence Yesenia in this manner.

It was a good thing she had emergency supplies tucked into a private bubble in her bedroom, for just this contingency.

Mama raised her brows. She knew about Yesenia's supply bubble. "You have sufficient food?"

"Enough to provide for me until tomorrow night." Yesenia paused. It might not be the *best* idea to catch a ride to the Fair tomorrow with Saul, and transit could expose her to spell traps.

Call Kirsten and ask for a ride?

Might be the best choice—and it would also let Yesenia know if Kirsten was trustworthy.

Meanwhile—

It's a good thing that my dresses are in the protective bubbles at the Fair.

If more than one member of the Family matrix wanted to break through Yesenia's spells and the protective matrices around the Fair to tamper with her dresses—their combined power plus the matrix would be enough to make it happen. Marisol had that much influence.

I had better check them first thing tomorrow morning.

That is, if Kirsten was willing to pick her up.

CHAPTER 4

THE WITCH STRIVING TO BECOME SOLO WILL FACE OPPOSITION

Opposition happens to any witch seeking out Solo status. If not from family and other witches, then the Mother of Magic herself may decide to try a witch's fitness to become Solo. No witch becomes Solo without undergoing some form of test of their dedication. The greater the test the Mother provides, the greater the Solo candidate's potential will be.

The Handbook for Newly Solo Witches, Second Edition

"THERE YOU ARE!" MARISOL CROWED THE NEXT MORNING, AS Yesenia tiptoed toward the front door. She sat up from her position on the living room couch, afghan wrapped around her.

Yesenia sighed and turned to face her aunt.

Did she stay up all night just to catch me?

"Yes, Auntie?"

"Is Saul taking you to and from the Fair today?"

"No, Auntie. This evening is the Tapestry Sing. Will you be there?"

33

Marisol snorted. "We have an urgent commission to finish today. You need to stay *here* and aid us with your strength. I called Saul to let him know. He can pick you up at lunchtime."

Yesenia tightened her lips. "I have obligations as the Fair Crown this morning, Auntie. I can't shirk them."

How dare she interfere!

"Fool." Marisol's face twisted, the pale shadow of her daemon overlaying it. "Who are you to think you could dare become Solo? The Family *needs* you, Yesenia—"

Even as Yesenia's stomach clenched—*something's wrong*—Kirsten's daemon brushed against Yesenia.

We're here, it said. Then flinched back. *Ouch!*

Be right there, Yesenia replied. She hurried to the door and grabbed the handle. It flared bright white. "Ow!" She jerked her hand back.

"I *told* you we had an urgent commission to finish today, and that you are needed. As Family Second, I *command* you!"

The Bright Star daemon quickly became *aware.*

This is not right, it hissed. *There is a wrongness in this place.*

What was Marisol trying to do, ruin the Fair? Yesenia whirled to face her aunt, summoning her personal daemon while simultaneously soothing Bright Star.

"Do you *want* to turn our Fair into a Lost Fair?" she hissed at her aunt. "Are you so bound in your jealousy that you would endanger all of us, even the Family matrix, just to force me to submit to your will?"

"Surely it's not that serious—" But that sense of *wrongness* radiating from Marisol expanded, feeling more and more threatening.

Do you need help? Kirsten asked through her daemon.

I don't think so, but be ready.

Yesenia summoned *copper* and hurled it at Marisol. She screeched and fell back on the couch. Yesenia reached for the door knob again. Cool, this time. She ran out of the house and jumped into the passenger seat of Kirsten's sedan.

"What's wrong?" Kirsten's brows furrowed with concern. "There was a lot of power flaring, and it didn't feel right."

"My aunt." Yesenia shook her head. "She tried to stop me from coming until this afternoon. Even called Saul and made arrangements for him to pick me up at lunchtime instead of this morning."

"What?" Kirsten's jaw dropped as she stared at Yesenia. "Doesn't she understand?"

"Hurry up and *go,*" Yesenia said. "I need to get away from here. Fast."

Kirsten's lips tightened. She backed the car out of the driveway, and sped down the street, slightly faster than was safe given the neighborhood, but right now Yesenia didn't care.

She didn't relax in her seat until they were several blocks away. Then her phone buzzed. Yesenia checked the number. Mama.

"Yesenia, what have you *done*?" Mama wailed.

"Something's not right with Aunt Marisol. She tried to stop me from leaving just now." Yesenia paused. "Did I hurt her badly when I threw magic at her?" she asked in a much smaller voice.

"She will recover." Mama's voice dropped in return. "What did she do?"

Yesenia gulped. "Mama, she tried to *command* me. As Family Second." Now she thought to check her aching palm. "She heated the door knob. There's a burn on my hand. Not bad, but—"

Mama inhaled sharply. "Oh *no.* What color was the magic?"

"White." Now Yesenia realized there was even more wrong. *White* was not the usual color of Marisol's magic—she usually cast spells in a warm, buttercup yellow. Why hadn't she noticed that then? "Mother of Magic. Mama, I didn't even think about that. What kind of magic is that sort of pale, pale white?"

"Not good."

"Is she—all right?"

"Listen."

Yesenia strained to hear. Someone was screaming and ranting in the background, spewing gibberish that wasn't Spanish, English, Mixtec, or Nahuatl. The words sent chills down her spine.

Do not listen! both her personal daemon and the Bright Star daemon warned.

"Mama. Both my daemons say not to listen further."

"I was afraid of that." Mama groaned. "Yesenia. Check your spells, carefully. Check your entries. Check everything. Tomas is calling an exorcist right now." Another pause. "My dear daughter. Do not come home until Fair is over. I do not know if this incursion came from outside or if it came in using you as cover. And if you do not win Fair Crown—do not come home at all."

Yesenia gulped. "Mama—"

"You were certain that you have the ability to go Solo. Well. It appears that you must either go Solo—or renounce your daemon. Marisol's actions have cast you out of the matrix. You're not safe here, unless you're Solo—or unmagicked."

"I'm sorry, Mama."

"Succeed. For the survival of our family matrix. Because it's clear now—if you fail, then the Fair will fail. And if the Fair fails —all of us are at risk. Do not come home if you fail."

"Mama—"

Mama hung up. Yesenia groaned and buried her head in her hands.

"Is everything all right?" Kirsten asked.

Yesenia rubbed her face, shuddering. Then she sat up and leaned her head against the back of her seat.

"Mama just told me not to come home until Fair is over. They're calling an exorcist to deal with Aunt Marisol." Yesenia choked back a sob. Much as she had wanted to be free of Family entanglements—

Not like this.

"Wow. You can stay with me."

"Thanks, Kirsten." Yesenia trembled, and blinked back tears. "Aunt Marisol was using *white* magic, when her magic is usually yellow. And there was a pale overlay when she summoned her daemon—"

Kirsten gasped. "The Curse of the Pale Wraith. By the Mother, Yeni, that's *bad*."

Mother of Magic, Mama needs to know that! Why didn't I—

Because the Pale Wraith blocked knowledge of it to those who were directly exposed. Which meant Mama *wouldn't know* either.

Yesenia quickly called her mother.

Her number was blocked. Yesenia stared at her phone. "I've been cut off," she said, her voice very small now.

Kirsten reached over and patted Yesenia's arm. "We'll figure something out, Yeni."

"I didn't realize it was the Pale Wraith—I need to call Saul." Yesenia punched his quick link.

Blocked.

"He's blocked me too," she whispered. "Mama told me to check everything. My exhibits. Not to come home if I don't win Fair Crown, because if I fail—we all fail. Kay, what has happened?"

"Could it be that strange witch's doing?"

"She swore loyalty to me for this Fair. The Fair daemon witnessed it. She comes from a Lost Fair, and offered assistance."

"Sounds to me like you—no, *we*—need to have a little chat with our newest member of the Fair." Kirsten's grim tone startled Yesenia, and she glanced at her friend. Kirsten's thin lips were set tight. "Because if she has done you wrong, if she has sworn wrong—I will make her pay."

Yesenia exhaled a ragged breath, reassured by Kirsten's quick support.

Things had seemed so bright and wonderful yesterday.

How could they have gone so wrong, so fast?

YESENIA DARTED OUT OF KIRSTEN'S CAR THE MOMENT KIRSTEN stopped, pausing only to grab her things before she sprinted to the static Exhibit Hall, heart pounding as she ran.

"Wait for me!" Kirsten yelled. "Yeni, slow down!"

But Yesenia couldn't pause, even for Kirsten.

She had to know, now.

The door to the Exhibit Hall wasn't unlocked yet, but as Fair Crown, Yesenia had the power to compel any door on the Fairgrounds to open for her. She rested her hand on the doorknob and it turned. She opened the door partway and left it ajar so that Kirsten could follow. Skittering through the tables and dividers, she finally spotted her exhibits.

A woman's simple and inexpensive formal dress, augmented by magic to sparkle when worn. A young girl's play outfit in white and green, the top with the image of a horse that galloped and whinnied when its wearer ran. A business suit that adjusted its color to match the wearer's complexion. Another one, that could be magically programmed to augment its wearer's emotions for up to an hour before the spell needed to be renewed. A hat and scarf set that set its warmth based on temperature. Protective shielding hats that created a bubble to repel rain, wind, and temperature extremes, that lasted a year instead of six months.

All ideas that she had discussed with Kirsten.

All concepts they hoped to integrate into their boutique, once they became Solo and earned the certification to use magic commercially, apart from a family matrix.

Yesenia extended her hands shakily and began to check the status of her spells.

"Is everything all right?" Kirsten asked, finally catching up with her.

"You best check your own items," Yesenia said absently. "Then we'll swap, and confirm. So far, so good."

"Got it." Kirsten went to her exhibits, two dividers down.

They *had* hoped to gain some interest in their designs at Bright Star Fair, then at State. Buyers for several magic-augmented clothing lines frequently surveyed the Fairs for that reason. But if their work had been tampered with—

Yesenia exhaled with relief as her spells glowed bright *copper*. All clear.

"I'm good," Kirsten called. "And you?"

"The same. But we'd better check each other."

They changed locations. Yesenia scrutinized Kirsten's designs closely—more coats, bags and purses than Yesenia had made.

All clear.

Another deep exhale.

"Now what?" Kirsten frowned. "Should we talk to the Exhibits Superintendent?"

"Absolutely, as well as Rosalee." Yesenia brushed back a strand of hair that had fallen into her face. "If this is part of an attack on the Fair—we'll need protection until the Sing. But first, we'd better check our Sing and Style Revue outfits."

Kirsten's lips tightened grimly. They left the Exhibit Hall. Yesenia hesitated. Should she wait until they had talked to the Superintendent before extending a greater protection spell over the Exhibit Hall, or should she do it now?

Activating *protection* would keep everyone out until she approved their presence.

Better safe than sorry.

Yesenia reached into her spell bag and pulled out a predesigned working that just needed the last tweaks to become a strong protective design. One of the tools she always carried, because there wasn't always time to create a full spell from scratch. She smacked it on the door, then traced the remaining elements, whispering *protect* to activate it.

The spell webbing glowed *copper*. Then tendrils extended out from the base working, stretching beyond the door.

Kirsten raised her brows. "Girl, that's one *powerful* spell."

"It needs to be. Come on, we'd better make sure our dresses are all right."

This time, Yesenia didn't run, but walked fast as they ducked and dodged through the livestock area and then the concessions. While the Exhibit Hall was on the edge of the Fairgrounds, the tent containing the Style Revue and, eventually, the Tapestry was at the center. A building next to it was the holding and changing area for the Sing and Style outfits.

This door was already unlocked. Yesenia and Kirsten exchanged frowns. They went inside. Dividers separated the areas for Style and Sing.

Style was the first set of dividers. Yesenia went to the bubble that contained her Style dress. She ran her finger down the bubble to open a slit, and slid inside. For this competition, she had chosen the Historical Costume division, replicating one of Elizabeth I of England's elaborate dresses, including the spells that Elizabeth had entwined in the embroidery, in homage to She who had been the Mother of Magic.

No problems with this dress.

Yesenia slipped out of that bubble, sealing it and adding additional safeguards. Then she went to the section containing the Sing outfits. Shadow was already there, frantically poking at a bubble. She whirled to face Yesenia.

"I can't open my bubble!"

"What?" Yesenia hurried to her bubble. Her usual marker was obscured, but this was the space she always used.

It didn't open.

"Kirsten!" Yesenia yelled. "Come here, fast!"

"What's wrong?" Kirsten spotted Shadow and frowned. "*You*. Of course."

"That's not the issue. Neither of us can open our bubbles. Can you open yours?"

Kirsten's mouth dropped open and she glanced back and forth between Shadow and Yesenia. They nodded.

Kirsten marched over to her bubble and tried to open it.

Nothing.

"No," Shadow moaned, shaking her head. "This is how it started at my Fair." She gulped. "Maybe we should check all of the bubbles. Maybe the outfits have just been moved around. Your bubbles are like ours were—no way to tell whose things are whose if the markers are obscured, because they hold in the magic so well."

"Was that what happened at your Fair?"

"Someone moved the bubbles around and blocked our bubble accesses. I needed to use the Fair daemon to open the Sing bubbles for everyone. And then—" she closed her eyes, shuddering. "We lacked power to defend the Tapestry when it was attacked at Fair opening."

"Mother of Magic, *no*," Kirsten murmured. "Did you have an appearance of the Pale Wraith as well?"

Shadow's eyes widened and she shook her head.

Kirsten and Yesenia exchanged looks. "The Wraith has appeared within my family matrix," Yesenia whispered. "The Family Second is affected. I can't go home until Fair is done—and not at all, if I fail to win Fair Crown."

"That is *bad*," Shadow said. "Look. Let's check all the bubbles."

Several trials revealed that the outfits had, indeed, been moved around. Yesenia found her Sing dress and slipped inside the bubble. She brought the Bright Star Fair daemon out to check it.

The Fair daemon chirped and purred as it flowed through the dress and its spells, making Yesenia giggle with its happiness. Then it eased back into its place within Yesenia.

She exhaled with relief and left the bubble, sealing it. Her marker reappeared.

Good.

"We need to let the others know that the bubbles have been moved." Kirsten frowned. "But who would do this?"

"A betrayer." Shadow scowled. "A betrayer who was interrupted in the process of sealing the bubbles, so that you would have needed to use the Fair daemon to open them for others, Yesenia. They only had time to move the bubbles and obscure the markers, not block them so it would be difficult for anyone other than you using the Fair daemon to open them."

"Who would that be?" Yesenia rubbed her chin thoughtfully. She couldn't think of anyone right away who would be so— petty.

"Someone close to the Fair," Shadow said. "Someone with magic, not a Typical. I came here early to check my outfits, because of what I remembered from my Fair. I felt diffused magic, nothing that could lead to identifying the culprit."

"Well, it should be all right now," Kirsten said.

"No." Shadow bristled. "I made that mistake, too!" She turned to Yesenia. "You need to find someone trustworthy, without magic. Have them check people in and out of the Sing and Style sections, as well as warning people that the Sing bubbles have been moved. And have a non-magical person in here, watching the Sing outfits."

"So several people," Yesenia said thoughtfully. "All right. Rosalee in here. Jeffrey for the men's side. And Sally to check everyone in and out."

Rosalee, Jeffrey, and Sally. The superintendents and assistant superintendents for this section of the Fair. Yesenia could already imagine their objections, especially from Sally.

Shadow's right, the Fair daemon said. *And it will not weaken me for you to bring me out to convince them, if necessary.*

Let's hope that isn't the case, Yesenia said. *I want you strong and powerful for the birth of your Tapestry!*

Bright Star purred and settled back into its coils; the gravid lump that was the unborn Tapestry even larger than it had been yesterday. Yesenia studied it. *Much* bigger than last year's Tapestry.

It would be one of the best Tapestries ever—that is, if more incidents like this didn't happen before tonight's Sing to sap the Fair daemon's strength.

~

"So what do we tell the other witches?" Kirsten wrung her hands.

The three of them sat at a picnic table near the Style Revue tent, after Yesenia had called Rosalee to tell her what had happened. So far, they were the only primary Sing participants who had arrived at the Fair. Now they were waiting for the others, to warn them.

"Just that the Sing outfits have been moved around and the markers obscured. Call it a prank," Shadow said. "That will annoy people but not get them afraid or mad."

"But if there *is* someone close to us who is doing this, shouldn't people know?" Kirsten fretted.

No. Bright Star appeared on the table top. It remained coiled around its gravid bulk, only raising its head and flicking its tongue. *Fear is worse, and if it is known that the Pale Wraith has touched the Fair Crown, you will lose confidence in the Fair Crown's ability to perform.*

Shadow and Kirsten's eyes widened, and they pulled back. Both bowed low to the daemon.

"Wow. Fair daemon doesn't usually appear to anyone who isn't the Crown," Kirsten whispered. "Bright Star, I am honored."

"I wish *my* Fair daemon had been this wise," Shadow said. "Maybe my Fair wouldn't have become Lost."

"So what *should* we say to the other witches?" Yesenia asked Bright Star. "They'll be angry and suspicious of everyone. I would think that would be just as problematic as being afraid."

The Bright Star Fair daemon turned its gaze upon her. *Someone moved the outfits, as Shadow the Question said. You can suggest that possibly another witch not involved with Style decided to play a practical joke on the Singers—it has been known to happen. Laugh and make it light, but be firm that you are taking precautions.*

Shadow tilted her head. "Other witches pull these pranks on the Singers? I've never heard of that happening before."

Bright Star chuckled. *All of you are very young. Yes, joking and pranks used to be much more common, back in the days when the world was slower and entities like the Pale Wraith were unknown to witches. Now*—it flickered its tongue and hissed before continuing. *Fun is not as common as it used to be. Magic has become deathly serious, and lost its sense of play, joy, and wonder. It has become a means for profit and power—to magic's detriment. We were supposed to bring happiness and fun!*

Yesenia bit her lip. "Bright Star is right. I remember bigger celebrations during Solstices when I was little. Wilder. I used to spy on them."

"Grandfather often complains about the focus on power in our family matrix meetings," Kirsten said. "He's told me stories about the big parties at Solstices. They sound like fun."

Shadow pressed her lips together and shook her head. "Survival has always been the focus for my family," she said softly.

Because of the injustices your family has suffered over the years. Bright Star gently nudged Shadow's hand, then reared up to stare in her eyes. Shadow sniffled, not looking away, until Bright Star turned its head, releasing her.

Witches courting power and status instead of trying to ease the burdens of all people. That gives openings to beings like the Pale Wraith, Bright Star continued. *Too many family matrices chase profit and not well-being. That's led to the loss of Fairs—but the loss of Shadow's Fair—now Nameless—has been a great blow to witchkind.* Sorrow tinged its voice. *It was one of my closest kin in age and power. Since it has fallen, I am the next target for the destroyers. If I go down—witchkind may die with me.*

"Why does someone want to destroy Magic Fairs?" Shadow whispered. "Even though my Fair was next oldest, everyone loved it. There *was* joy there. Not every magic creation was about utility."

And that is what we need. Bright Star flicked its tongue. *Things like Yesenia's shirt, where a little one's dream of riding a horse becomes real to them. Too much magic these days is focused on useful things. We need to have fun as well—but the destroyers want to rid the world of magical fun.*

"How do we stop them?" Yesenia asked. "I will do whatever it takes, Bright Star."

"So will I," Kirsten said.

"And I," Shadow whispered.

Cultivate fun, happiness, and joy as you Sing my new Tapestry, Bright Star said. It turned its head and nudged its gravid bulge. *I am doing my best to create the finest Tapestry ever. But I depend on you three to make it successful. Collaborate. Trust each other. Support each other. Yesenia, Shadow, and Kirsten. The three of you must be my greatest defense. But perform my defense in joy, not fear.*

The three women eyed each other. Then Yesenia put her right hand out, palm up. Kirsten rested her hand on Yesenia's, and last, slowly and reluctantly, Shadow.

"We *will* work together. Right?" Yesenia demanded.

She met first Kirsten's eyes, then Shadow's, waiting for the nod of assent.

When it came, she smiled.

They clasped their hands. Bright Star sent a wave of happiness over them.

The three of you are a benefit to witchkind. Then Bright Star faded.

The three of them beamed at each other, before exhaling as Bright Star's projection faded.

"We will bring joy, not just to Bright Star Fair, but beyond." Yesenia drew a deep breath before she continued. "I know this is asking a lot—especially from you, Shadow, because I don't know what resources you have." She paused, gathering her thoughts before continuing. "This is short notice. But if we could put together outfits and a comic routine for the Style group presentation division—a late entry—that could help us disguise a further protective routine for the Fair."

Kirsten pursed her lips. "That could work. Group presentation is tomorrow morning, first thing. We need to pull together designs and a routine quickly. Shadow, where are you staying? I have the costume resources, and we could devise the routine now."

Shadow looked down. "I—don't really have a place to stay. I've been camping around the Fair."

"That stops, right now," Kirsten said. "Yesenia is going home with me tonight. So are you."

"But—but—" Shadow gestured at herself. "I'm Black. You're white."

"It doesn't matter," Kirsten said. "Not in my family."

"Who *is* your family?" Shadow asked.

Yesenia pressed her lips together to keep from reacting before Kirsten told Shadow.

"I'm a Rogers," Kirsten said.

Shadow's eyes widened. "A *Rogers*? *The* Rogers? The County Commissioner? The Judge?"

Kirsten nodded slowly.

"Then—why are the two of you bothering with all of this?" Shadow gestured. "You, especially, Kirsten. You can *buy* your way into Solo."

Kirsten and Yesenia exchanged glances. Then Kirsten sighed.

"My family is old and traditional among witchkind," Kirsten said. "They want me to know the old ways of doing things. They want me to earn my position. And yes. Judge Rogers is my father and Commissioner Rogers is my uncle."

Shadow shook her head. "I don't believe it. I'm hanging out with a Rogers."

"Believe it." Kirsten smiled, then grew more solemn. "But be prepared. Dad and Uncle may want to talk to you about what happened at your Fair—and what's happening at Bright Star."

"If I can," Shadow murmured. "I have—some restrictions."

"Dad may be able to loosen some of them."

Hope briefly flared in Shadow's eyes.

Then she sighed. "I wish that what you say will turn out to be right. But I have had too many bad things happen in my life to be too positive about it."

"Remember what the Fair daemon said." Kirsten tightened her hands on Shadow's. "We need to be positive. We need to visualize success." She grinned. "I won't let Yesenia fall into doom casting. Looks like I need to do the same for you."

Yesenia exhaled with relief. Bright Star seemed to trust Shadow, and Kirsten was convinced.

So perhaps they were right. She needed to trust her daemon's judgment.

CHAPTER 5

THE WITCH WHO WOULD KEEP FAIR CROWN MUST CONTROL THE FAIR DAEMON

E*ven the oldest and most controlled Fair daemons strive to overcome the Crown who manages them as their time to birth the Tapestry approaches. The Crown must absolutely not yield to the whims of the Fair daemon at this time, trustworthy though they are on other occasions. Once the Sing begins, the Crown must control the Fair daemon's impulse to rush the process—or else lose all.*

The Fair Crown's Handbook, Ninth Edition

ROBING FOR THE FAIR CROWN AND HER CLOSE ATTENDANTS happened in separate rooms of the Fair Office, where the Sing would begin.

"You *had* to leave robing until the last minute!" Kirsten scolded as she fussed at the complex weaving of magic and fabric which traced down the long sleeves of Yesenia's Sing outfit. *Copper*, yellow, and red swaths intertwined and almost seemed to vibrate around each other in both the tightly-fitting sheath dress and the gauzy, flowing robe that swirled around

49

Yesenia, agitated by the invisible but roiling presence of the Bright Star Fair daemon.

Yesenia rolled her eyes. "I had to walk Maria through the parts of the Sing she missed, because she was late to rehearsal."

"Yeah. What's that about?" Kirsten grumbled as the robe's fabric twitched out of her hand. "Darn this fabric. It has a mind of its own."

"Agreed."

"Maria's getting later and later every day, it seems."

"None of the daemons seemed to be bothered about Maria's absence."

"Including Shadow's?"

Yesenia winced. "She was busy making the last-minute amendments to her outfit so that it would match ours. They didn't meet."

"So that's why Shadow's not acting as Second Attendant! I could use her help."

There *had* been some complaints about Yesenia appointing Shadow as her Second Attendant during the Sing rehearsal. But Maria hadn't shown up until the last third of practice today, and Shadow *had* won the Style Crown at State Fair last year, so she outranked anyone else who might aspire to that position.

Especially Maria.

But Yesenia didn't say that, for fear of provoking Kirsten to a further rant about Maria's absence and Shadow's alterations. Kirsten was already edgy about helping Yesenia robe before she did her own preparation—normal for her before any Sing. Even before they had earned their titles as Advanced Witches, even when they were just followers supporting the Fair Crowns, Kirsten had fretted about doing the Sing perfectly.

Add to that the need for this robe to go on *just right*, with none of the lines of *copper* crossing, and Kirsten's nervousness was to be expected.

But understanding and expecting Kirsten's behavior didn't make keeping Bright Star manageable any easier. The Fair daemon strained at its bonds, wanting to be free. Wanting to birth the Tapestry.

"There!" Kirsten stepped back. "Finally. Everything's straight." She glanced at the clock. "Just in time! I need to get dressed and give you space to assume the Crown."

"Thank you."

Now that she was alone, Yesenia closed her eyes for a moment, to prepare her thoughts and eliminate outside concerns.

Forget the Pale Wraith. Forget the Cruz family matrix. Forget Saul. Forget the worries about Shadow. Forget the concern about becoming Solo. Forget everything except Bright Star and the Fair.

Then she opened her eyes.

With a snap, she summoned the spell mirror that would help her monitor and control the manifestation of Bright Star within her.

Drew in one breath, filling herself with the steadiness of stone.

Second breath, grounding herself.

Third breath, tuning into the flow of magic that interacted with her personal daemon and the agitated Bright Star Fair daemon. She closed her eyes again, and visualized the strands of *copper* winding through her dress and robe. Yesenia channeled her personal daemon into those threads, strengthening herself for the onslaught of power that Bright Star would soon release.

"*Activate,*" Yesenia murmured.

The sweet scent of lilacs that signified her daemon momentarily teased her nostrils, announcing its awakening through her sense of scent. A brief flowery flavor like her abuela's favorite violet pastille candies that Yesenia used to steal when younger filled her mouth. Then sound blared. The voices in the next cubicle momentarily overwhelmed both Yesenia and her daemon and she fought back the urge to clap her hands over her ears. The room flared *too bright* and even the slightest brush of air across her hand felt heavy.

Then Yesenia's senses compensated for her new, hightened awareness. Sound, touch, and vision no longer overloaded her perception of the world around her. A sensation of steadiness, of the strength to face whatever might come her way, settled upon her.

I am Yesenia the Steadfast. I will prevail.

She raised her hands.

"Activate," she repeated.

This time, waves of bright, glowing *copper* washed over her doubled self as she and her personal daemon raised their shared magic. The tangy taste of *copper* filled her mouth. Warmth oozed up from her fingertips and into her core.

Yesenia breathed in, careful to balance the hot, fiery burn of *copper* with the cooler air to keep the magic from blazing out of control within her. This close to Solo, with Bright Star roaring strong, ready to give birth to a new Tapestry, it was possible to burn herself badly.

Other witches had failed in just this manner when attempting their third Fair Crown, by growing impatient and not completely stabilizing themselves before raising their Fair daemons.

Yesenia took three more deep breaths as *copper* settled into place, her whole being resonating with *copper*. She gazed into the spell mirror. *Copper* twined up the sleeves of her dress and robe, making the red and gold shimmer. *Copper* lines wove and glowed on her dress.

I am ready, she whispered to Bright Star.

A bitter, metallic taste filled her mouth as the Crown awoke and took shape on Yesenia's head.

Gold glimmered against the dark brown of her hair. *Gold, silver*, and *copper* threads writhed into place on her dress and robe. *Copper* shimmered even brighter as *gold* and *silver* joined it and the Crown became more solid. More power flooded into Yesenia, evoking that bright thrill she had first felt two years ago when she won the Crown at the end of the Fair.

As Bright Star writhed and tried to move *beyond* her, Yesenia grasped it hard.

No. Not yet, she ordered. She stared into her spell mirror, focusing on those brightly glowing strands of *gold* and *silver*, making *copper* grow and become more dominant.

Yesenia breathed in the essence of Bright Star and the Fair. It pulsated through her veins and arteries, left a burnt caramel taste in her mouth that whispered of the approach of autumn while embracing these last high days of summer.

Bright Star yanked at Yesenia. It wanted to race out the door to begin her Sing. It pulled at her feet to get them to move, jerked at her fingers to make them twitch in the summoning sequence.

Wait, Yesenia commanded.

Go. Now, Bright Star whined.

We are not yet ready, Yesenia answered.

Bright Star sent a smoky taste to her tongue, accented by the scent of burnt wood and grass. *I burn. I burn to be born.*

We. Must. Wait.

Her body heated as Bright Star kept pushing. Yesenia held steady. Oh, this year's Tapestry would be *great*—but she had to hold her ground and not let Bright Star rush. It was still quixotic and wild, not yet ready to submit to Yesenia's will. This was not the wise advisor of earlier in the day, but a Fair daemon ready to give birth to the Tapestry it carried, impatient to reveal its newest form and glory.

To let it dominate now would destroy the Fair.

Just when she thought she could stand no more heat, it faded. Impatience flowed away as Bright Star's majesty manifested in the spell mirror, red threads glimmering around the *gold* of the Fair Crown, shining so bright that it was hard to focus. Bright Star manifested itself in its full gravid glory, coiling around Yesenia's torso and extending up her back to encircle the Crown.

Yesenia smiled at their reflection. Then she snapped away the spell mirror.

Are we ready to Sing? she asked Bright Star.

Bright Star hummed happily. *We are ready. And may this be one of my best Tapestries ever, Fair Crown. We do good work!*

Then let us go forth.

Yesenia stepped out of the office at the end of the hallway.

"Court, are you ready?" she called.

"Just a minute!" Maria yelled.

"*I am ready.*" Shadow stood in the doorway of the office she had used as a changing room. Yesenia admired what Shadow had done to modify her dress—at last year's State Style competition, that dress had been primarily greens and blues, with Shadow's magic glowing in bright red *iron*.

Shadow had changed the color scheme of this dress to reflect Bright Star. Red was too bright, too much like the shades of her *iron* magic. But orange and gold with black trim marked this sleeveless wrap dress, her *iron* outlining shapes that resembled falling autumn leaves.

"And so am I." Kirsten appeared in her doorway, her colors pale green marked with yellow stripes, her *bronze* magic creating the shape of alder leaves just beginning to turn. Her Style Crown glimmered in silver and *bronze*, perfectly in order. No daemon stirred in that crown—the lesser Fair Crowns were but reflections of the glory of the Fair and the one who wore them. Her dress was a sheath with long sleeves, like Yesenia's.

"Here I am." Maria stepped out. "I'm sorry it took so long. My sleeves wouldn't untangle." The steel Design Crown sat at a slight angle on her dark hair.

"Crown's not right," Kirsten said.

"I know, it didn't want to cooperate," Maria fussed. "My hair kept slipping out. Kirsten, can you fix it? You have the touch for this Crown."

"Of course." Kirsten crossed the hallway and delicately adjusted the combs holding Maria's crown in place. "Ow!" She made a face. "Your hair is all static-y."

"I'm sorry. I don't know why my hair is so wild today. Thank

shoulders. "Bright Star Fair!" she called. "Welcome this addition to our Fair! Welcome Shadow the Question, last year's State Style Crown, into our mix!"

"We welcome Shadow the Question!" the Courts shouted back.

If any were hesitant, the others drowned them out.

"Shadow the Question, please assume your State Style Crown and take your place in my Court."

Shadow curtseyed to Yesenia. Then she turned to the Courts and curtseyed to them. "I thank you for your acceptance and bestow my blessings upon Bright Star Fair. I will honor my role and hold it with joy."

Shadow raised her hands and the State Style Crown, glowing malachite green, manifested itself. A distinct *click* resonated through Yesenia as Shadow set the Crown on her head, completing the Fair Procession in a way that made Yesenia catch her breath.

We were missing a piece! Mother of Magic, thank you!

Curiouser and curiouser.

Shadow returned to her position behind Kirsten and Maria. Yesenia turned and reached for the wards that were supposed to exclude all but the approved from the tent. As she dismissed the wards, a tingle began in her feet and worked its way up her legs, her torso, her arms, radiating through her fingertips and hair. Tiny pinpricks of power surged into a great wave of powerful magic that crashed over her. Sweet *copper* burned through Yesenia until she could no longer hold it within her body. She spread her arms wide, as if carrying an invisible beach ball. The *presence* of the Bright Star Fair daemon flowed into that space, glowing bright gold and white.

Tobias and the musicians began the Processional for the First Sing.

Yesenia stepped forward on her lucky right foot, still holding Bright Star high as she danced four steps forward. Then she dropped her arms and Bright Star wrapped itself around Yesenia as she began to Sing the old words, the language she barely understood, the voice of the land and the magic it contained.

She led the dance into the tent, hands weaving sinuously around her as Bright Star glowed even brighter than ever. They danced the four corners of the tent as Tobias and the musicians retreated to their stage and picked up those instruments. Steel drums began a calypso beat.

After dancing the corners, Yesenia capered over to the musicians' stage, bowing low to them. Then she approached the runway steps, kneeling to awaken the power held latent in them until now, holding her hands over them as Bright Star's power flashed first into the steps, then the runway, then the stage. Bright copper, gold, and red lights glowed around the edges of the panels, the steps, and the stage.

The musicians paused as magic wove itself around them and their stage. Then their music changed rhythm.

It is time.

Yesenia marched up the steps and down the runway to the main stage. The others followed on the ground, lining up along the stage as Yesenia halted before the Tapestry's hanging site.

She visualized the image she and Bright Star had been cultivating since last Fair. The Grounds at peace, magic unfolding in predictable and precise patterns. No animals sickening. No spells gone awry, no burned food, no harsh words of rebuke or envy. Crisp morning excitement as competitors and livestock prepared for a show day. Fatigue by dusk as the dark blues and blacks of a high summer evening glided slowly over them, exhibitors collapsing with satisfied fatigue at the end of the day.

Holding that vision perfect in her brain, Yesenia sang a full, deep A, breathing her vision out to take shape in a single shimmering bubble that formed between her hands as Bright Star twined around her fingers. The musicians picked up that A. The Court joined, followed by the others.

The bubble glided from Yesenia's fingers. It stretched into a long, thin, translucent tube. Bright Star and Yesenia guided it to the holder. They fastened it gently on the left hook, then the middle, and at last the right.

Then everything glared white as Bright Star screamed, giving birth to the Tapestry. Yesenia squinched her eyes tightly shut. When she opened them, Bright Star coiled around the edges of the unfolded but still shimmering Tapestry.

Yesenia began the final Song. The exact words she used for this spell didn't matter, as long as the correct meanings were expressed.

Welcome.

"Welcome to the Bright Star Fair." She traced a figure in the air, and the Tapestry undulated, the glow diminishing into plain gray.

Blessings.

"Bright blessings on all who enter." Memories of Great-Aunt Eufalia, who had been one of the greatest Bright Star Fair Crowns, colored this section of the spell. Eufalia had bolstered Yesenia's confidence after her defeat at State last year had shaken her.

Peace. Prosperity.

"May Bright Star be a place of peace and prosperity for another year." It had been Eufalia's suggestion after Yesenia won Fair Crown to combine the two elements this year, especially after the reports of several Lost Fairs. And since Aunt Eufalia had helped restore a Lost Fair—

Fairness. Safety.

"May all competitions be honest and true; may all be free from harm; may no magic escape to endanger the Typicals."

The last elements the spell needed.

"So will it be."

BOOM!

Tobias pounded hard on his big bass drum, keeping up a steady patter as the plain gray Tapestry fabric blazed in bright color, Bright Star twisting through it until it took its final form.

Oohs and ahhhs of appreciation broke out from behind her as the features came clear.

The Tapestry stabilized into an elegant portrait of the Fair, only a Victorian version instead of modern. Bright Star detached from the main portion of the Tapestry, and tucked itself into a little cave Yesenia had designed for its comfort in the lower right-hand corner. It coiled upon itself and settled in, golden eyes glowing watchfully.

Little figures moved on the Tapestry. Yesenia scrutinized it carefully. Had she been able to animate the most intricate details? She had tried and failed to do that last year. It wasn't until she conferred with Eufalia last winter that she knew how to do this.

She smiled as closer examination revealed its effectiveness. Then she turned to the others, spreading her arms wide.

"Come and see," she invited them.

It was done.

Would it be good enough to ensure she earned that last Fair Crown she needed to become Solo?

She wouldn't know until the Fair Committee's inspection tomorrow morning.

But for now—it was time to rejoice with her fellow witches.

The Tapestry was completed. The Fair had begun.

NEW, NON-WITCH GUARDS WERE SET OVER THE BUILDINGS containing the important Fair magical outfits and exhibits after the Sing. Yesenia walked around the Fair, inspecting all the wards, just in case.

The wards didn't warn me about Shadow's presence.

Something to worry about, because the next intruder might not have Shadow's positive intent.

Yesenia checked the wards around the Style tent, then had Kirsten and Shadow examine them. She would have had Maria look too, but she had disappeared back into the Fair Office to change, then scurried out when Yesenia, Kirsten, and Shadow reached the office.

"See you tomorrow!" Maria called back, hurrying toward the parking lot.

Yesenia hesitated before going inside to change. Her daemon stirred restlessly.

Something is not right.

Was that the *pop-pop-pop* sound that the exhaust of Saul's pickup sometimes made? Yesenia squinted toward the parking lot. Maria climbed into a pickup that pulled into the lot, not one that had been parked. It wasn't *quite* the color of Saul's pickup— but pickup colors could be glamoured, with enough magical power.

Saul by himself lacked that magic. But with Maria—

And that pickup sure sounded like his. Why would he be picking up Maria?

"Yeni, what's going on?" Kirsten popped back out to join Yesenia. "Let's get moving."

"Nothing. Probably." Yesenia gave her a quick smile. Why bother Kirsten over this? They already had enough to worry about.

Yesenia carefully tucked her Fair Sing dress back into its bubble, then grabbed her spell bag and the small overnight duffle she kept in a sealed cubicle here in the Fair Office, for emergency changes of clothing and makeup fixes.

Then she, Kirsten, and Shadow towed their bubbles back to the regular changing area. Tobias stood guard by the door, his arms crossed.

"We're keeping our instruments in here, too," he said. "My daemon is uneasy. Rosalee wanted me to check with you first, Yesenia, to make sure that you didn't mind us doing that."

"That's a good idea," Shadow said.

I spoke to Tobias's daemon, Bright Star said from its cave in the Tapestry. *I will be on guard here all night, but the Fair musi-*

cians should keep their instruments in a safe place. It will be easier for me.

"I agree," Yesenia said.

Tobias's face softened with relief. "Thank you, Yesenia. If someone tampered with our instruments...." His voice trailed off.

"Who's standing watch on the building?" Yesenia asked.

"Stephen," Tobias said, naming Rosalee's counterpart for the large animal division. "I'm just waiting for him to come back from setting up watches around the Fair." He rolled his eyes. "I'm sure the Fair Board will have something to say about the expense of added protection. But Rosalee and the others talked, and given that your family matrix has been touched by the Pale Wraith—it's a very good idea."

So who has been talking about that?

She hadn't *thought* her situation was common knowledge. Oh well. One thing after another. All she could do was proceed.

At last, it was time to walk to Kirsten's car. Yesenia had stalled as long as possible, because she didn't want to think about the situation at home. She, Shadow, and Kirsten wound through the parking lot, now mostly taken up by the campers connected to the livestock division. The grinding of Shadow's roller suitcase reminded Yesenia that her only supplies were in that small emergency duffle that she carried, along with her spell bag. She stopped to take a look inside of it, and sighed.

"I need to do laundry tonight. Kirsten, can I borrow something to sleep in?"

"Should we go by your house to get some more clothes?"

"I wouldn't do that," Shadow said. "Since the Pale Wraith has manifested in your family matrix, Yesenia, it's dangerous to get too close. Do you live near Yesenia, Kirsten?"

Yesenia snorted. "Are you serious? The Rogers family has money. The Cruz family—doesn't. In any case, it doesn't matter. I *can't* go back. I've been cut off from the Cruz family matrix.

Mama told me I can't go back unless I'm either Solo, or unmagicked."

"That's not good," Shadow said.

"All of my tools are at home." Yesenia shook her head as regret washed over her. "My fabric stash. My sewing machine. I have my spell bag, but nothing else."

"Could Saul get them for you?" Kirsten asked.

"I don't trust him," Yesenia said.

Not after what I thought I saw in the parking lot.

So why couldn't she just say that to Kirsten and Shadow? Unwillingness to face what was most likely her current reality?

"But he's been devoted to you. I've been kinda jealous that you had him," Kirsten said.

"Marisol said she called him to pick me up at noon." Yesenia tapped her fingers on the door. "How do I know he's safe? And besides—Papa was getting an exorcist to deal with Marisol. What if it didn't work? Could I trust anything from home?"

"That's true. And given that it's the Pale Wraith—Saul could come under its influence if he goes by the house."

"You need to be careful about boyfriends," Shadow said. "I thought my man was loyal to me, too. And then he was used to destroy my Fair."

"Was he the one who sealed the bubbles for your Fair's Sing outfits?" Yesenia asked, as they put their things into Kirsten's car.

"Yes." Shadow's voice was very quiet.

Yesenia pressed her lips together, worrying.

What if Marisol already influenced Saul? What if the Cruz family matrix was channeled through him to seal our Sing outfit bubbles, and we showed up before he could finish the job?

But Saul wouldn't do that to her—would he?

"Saul wouldn't hurt Yesenia. They've been engaged for two years," Kirsten said firmly.

"Do we know that he wouldn't hurt me, for certain?" Yesenia murmured, dreading to put the heaviness in her gut into words.

They climbed into the car.

"If you have any doubts, you're best off not coming in contact with him," Shadow said. "Until the Fair is over."

More weight in Yesenia's gut. Shadow would understand if she told them about what she might have seen in the parking lot.

So why couldn't she say anything about it?

"I don't intend to come in contact with him until after Fair."

"Good," Shadow said. After a few minutes, once they were driving through the upper-middle class neighborhood next to Kirsten's, she continued. "So, you have witches who are rich that participate in the Fair and other activities?"

"Of course," Kirsten said. "Not just as commissioners and judges. All of us in the area ruled by the Bright Star daemon contribute to the witch community. How else could you sustain a region's magic?"

"It wasn't that way where I lived," Shadow said softly. "Where my Fair—was—we didn't have many wealthy participants. They mostly considered themselves to be too good to participate in the Fair. Even the witches."

"Ah. So how *did* witches survive, much less the Fair?"

Bright Star had a lot of respect for Shadow's Fair. Did things change, so that the daemon isn't aware of them?

"That was—part of the problem," Shadow said. "Not all of the witches in our Fair's area were poor. But they had their own gatherings, and thought that those would be enough to renew the land's magic. One set of magic for the rich, another for the poor. Oh, they were good enough to judge *our* Fair, and assess *our* Fair's Tapestry, but only the very best from *our* Fair got to go to State. Or become Solo." Her voice sharpened. "But the other, lesser folk, either because we were poor or people of color? We weren't recognized. There were quotas. Lots of witches who could have gone Solo ended up affiliated with richer family matrices because they were forced into it. Most of those who went to State Fair and became Solo came from the rich folks' secret gatherings."

Yesenia glanced uneasily at Kirsten. Kirsten's lips tightened. Both of them had noticed issues with Fair administration judging over the past few years, but so far—there hadn't been any secret gatherings of rich witches within Bright Star's domain.

That we know of.

"That's troubling," Kirsten said. "What happened when your Fair came under attack?"

Shadow snorted derisively. Her voice turned harsh. "When the forces of destruction turned on us, I did my best to unify our people. We called on the others to join with us. But because they hadn't joined with the Fair, because they lacked the connection with our Fair daemon—" she shook her head. "I can't go back. No witch can return to that Fair's domain, and hope to keep their magic. The destruction spilled beyond the Fair and into those other gatherings."

Kirsten gulped. "You have to talk to my father and my uncle, then, Shadow. You *have* to. Because if Bright Star is a target—" Her voice trailed off.

Yesenia stared blindly out of the window.

She hadn't been prepared for this likelihood, and it showed.

What if I never can go back home?

What would she do?

WORRY ABOUT HER FUTURE SHADED YESENIA'S MOOD AS SHE followed Kirsten into the spacious Rogers home. It was an older, two-story mid-century modern rambler with a daylight basement. Unlike others in the same subdivision, the Rogers family had chosen comfort over style. *Welcome* washed over every visitor, unless they exhibited some characteristic that offended the Rogers' wards.

Kirsten was the youngest child of the family, and had taken over the basement area. This was where she and Yesenia worked on projects for their projected boutique. Her parents had an upstairs bedroom and office. So the three of them would have the basement all to themselves, with plenty of space. That didn't fret Yesenia as much as the question—where would she go after the Fair?

From Shadow's subdued quiet as they walked inside, Yesenia suspected she shared the same worries, only with more experience of being cast out.

"Hello, darling." Kirsten's mother Janna came out from the kitchen and hugged her. "Hi, Yesenia, and who is this?"

"Shadow," Kirsten said. "Her Fair is Lost, and Bright Star has taken her in."

"Oh my dear," Janna said, taking Shadow's hands. "I am so sorry to hear this. You are welcome in this house, for as long as you need a place to stay."

"Are you sure?" Shadow asked, her voice low. "You trust that I wouldn't do something dangerous because I come from a Lost Fair?"

"Bright Star took you in, and our house wards welcomed you," Janna said. "That's all I need to know."

Shadow blinked hard, freeing one hand to wipe her eyes.

"Yesenia needs a place to stay," Kirsten said. "There's been some problems."

Janna sighed. "Yes. The Senior Council knows. Rosalee informed us. Your father and your uncle want to talk to the three of you, Kirsten, so I'm glad that Shadow is here. They'll be here in an hour or so—the Council is still meeting."

The Council.

Shadow's face tightened and ice spiked through Yesenia's gut.

"Oh ladies, don't worry," Janna said reassuringly, projecting *welcome, happiness,* and *joy.* "None of you—all *three* of you—are in trouble. We heard that the Tapestry is absolutely gorgeous, and I'm *certain* that the Fair Committee will approve it tomorrow morning. No, while this has to do with Fair-related concerns, it's not because of anything you have done." She waved her hands. "Wally will be angry with me if I tell you more, but it's a good thing. Really. It is."

Kirsten silently led them downstairs. They stopped in the small living area, set up with a cutting table, cubicles for storage of fabric and completed items, two couches, a computer and writing space, two sewing machines, and a TV with several gaming systems attached to it.

Kirsten gestured to one door. "I need to clear things out of this bedroom for you, Shadow. Yesenia, you could take your usual room."

"Are you sure?" Shadow looked around the living area. "I don't mind sleeping on the floor."

"My mother would just *kill* me if I made you do that. You're my guest, and *both* of you are going to be here for a while. We need to be comfortable!"

"I'll help you clear the bedroom," Yesenia said.

"Me too," Shadow said.

"I need to put things away, anyway," Kirsten sighed, brushing a strand of blonde hair out of her eyes.

Usually, Yesenia would laugh about Kirsten's chronic clutter. Today, however, she just wanted to groan. She was tired and the prospect of mucking out the mess in that third bedroom exhausted her—but it needed to happen. She stifled the whimper she wanted to make, and set her duffle and her spell bag next to Shadow's.

The three of them dove into clearing the bedroom for Shadow's use. Most of the things that needed to be put away were fabrics and partially-completed items that needed to rest before their spells were completed.

As always, Yesenia's sour mood faded as she handled the fabrics and Kirsten's half-made items. Kirsten had an eye for beautiful colors and fabric patterns—one of her strengths. Shadow murmured happily over the luscious fabrics, sometimes taking a moment to admire this or that bolt or creation.

"I wish I could afford to work with beautiful material and create things like this," Shadow said wistfully as they neared the end of the bedroom clearout, studying one of Kirsten's bags. "I used to make wall hangings. Then I needed to put all my effort into competition outfits."

Kirsten stopped organizing her thread caddy. "Yesenia and I plan to open a boutique once we're both Solo."

"*Lucky.* If I could, I'd make art quilts. Not Tapestry-level quilts, but wall hangings and soft furnishings."

"Do you have any pictures of your work?" Yesenia asked.

Shadow fumbled for her phone. "All these pieces are gone. Lost along with my Fair. They're my real strength, not my outfits." A sad tone came into her voice. "Not much call for work like this, however." She handed the phone to Yesenia.

Kirsten looked over Yesenia's shoulder as she swiped through the pictures. "Shadow, that's *lovely*. What do you mean, there's not much call for work like this? I know buyers who would pay premium prices for these pieces."

Shadow's lips tightened. "You're kidding me."

"No. It's a matter of making connections—"

"And *connections* are important." Wallace Rogers, Kirsten's father, said as he came down the stairs. His brother Frederick followed.

Yesenia and Shadow straightened up as Kirsten went to greet her father and uncle. The aura of *Council* radiated from both men, a heavy, warm weight of *power* and *authority*. Even though Yesenia knew both men well, she had rarely seen them in their Council roles.

They were terrifyingly *strong* in these personas.

She and Shadow bowed low to the men.

"Ah, now, let's dispense with the formalities," Wallace said, gesturing toward the couches. "Ladies, let's sit and talk."

Yesenia sat on one couch, Kirsten on her left, Shadow on her right. Both women pressed close against her. Kirsten quivered, not quite as much as Shadow, but it was clear that Kirsten was also nervous. Even though the Council members sitting on the other couch across from them were her father and her uncle.

"Relax," Frederick said. "You three are not on trial."

"Kind of hard not to think so when a Commissioner and a Judge from the Council are wanting to talk to us." Shadow's voice trembled. "This feels like the interrogation I went through after my Fair became Lost."

"Understood," Wallace said. Then he straightened up and became fully Judge Rogers, assuming the aspect of Judge as Frederick assumed the aspect of Commissioner.

"We regret how the loss of Moonrise Fair was handled by those Judges and Commissioners," Commissioner Rogers said.

Shadow gulped. "It doesn't change the fact that it happened." She blinked hard.

Yesenia put an arm around Shadow, *feeling* the ache radiating from Shadow at the mention of her Fair.

Moonrise Fair. Oh. Mother of Magic. That was her Fair.

A powerful Fair, a powerful daemon, with a long history and almost as strong as Bright Star. Yesenia shivered.

"No," Judge Rogers said. "It does not. But our concern is with keeping Bright Star from falling into the same trap that Moonrise did. And, if possible, restoring Moonrise."

"I didn't think that was possible." Shadow blinked hard, her body trembling against Yesenia's. "I was told it was completely Lost."

"The fact that Moonrise's last Fair Crown still lives tells us that Moonrise can be recovered," Commissioner Rogers said.

"But the daemon is *gone!*" Shadow wailed. "I can't feel it anymore."

"My dear, if the daemon was completely gone, you would be dead," Judge Rogers said flatly. "A Fair Crown will not survive their daemon's banishment."

Shadow buried her head in her hands, shaking with tears. Silence fell as she cried.

At last Shadow raised her head. "I failed my Fair. I should have died with it."

"There would be no hope of bringing it back if you had died," Judge Rogers said. "It is good that you survived."

"But how can I bring it back?"

The Judge and the Commissioner shared a glance. Judge Rogers nodded to his brother. "Yours to explain, Fred."

"The Destroyers are gathering to attack Bright Star," Commissioner Rogers said. "Yesenia, we are investigating the manifestation of the Pale Wraith in your family matrix."

"Has it been exorcised?" she asked.

"We do not know yet. Your family has closed themselves off —as they should, when dealing with this threat."

"Then it should be all right?" Her voice quavered. "Bright Star, I mean."

"The Pale Wraith is not the only Destroyer to be concerned about," Commissioner Rogers said. "The Red Horseman also rises."

"*No*," Shadow wailed. "Not Jerome—"

"The Horseman does not ride that person here," Commissioner Rogers said. "You truly destroyed Jerome's ability to host any daemon while defending your Fair, Shadow. He can no longer be a host to the Horseman. It is why there is a hope of restoring Moonrise. But the Red Horseman and the Pale Wraith are not tied to any particular persons. We do not know who has taken on those aspects in order to destroy the Bright Star Fair. Your excellent Sing tonight did wonders toward making Bright Star strong. All the same—Bright Star is endangered."

"How do we protect it?" Yesenia couldn't keep a quaver out of her voice now. "Especially against both the Pale Wraith and the Red Horseman."

"It will take that rarest of alliances, a Solo Knot, in order to defeat the Destroyers. They have formed a Destroying Knot." An odd expression crossed Commissioner Rogers's face.

"But—we don't have a Solo Knot in Bright Star, Uncle Fred—

" Kirsten's voice trailed off as she stared at her uncle. "None of us are Solo!"

"None of you are Solo *yet*," Commissioner Rogers corrected. "You do not need to have earned your full Solo status to form a Solo Knot." He looked steadily at each of them in turn. "Kirsten. You have two Bright Star Style Crowns. You are one Crown away from becoming Solo eligible. Yesenia. You have two Bright Star Fair Crowns, and, like Kirsten, are one Crown away from your Solo status. Shadow, you have State Style Crown and Moonrise Fair Crown, so, like Kirsten and Yesenia, you are one Crown away from Solo eligibility."

"How does that help us now?" Yesenia gulped.

Judge Rogers and Commissioner Rogers stood.

"The three of you have the core strengths required to form a Solo Knot," Commissioner Rogers said. "You will prove your worthiness to become Solo by successfully forming the Knot and defending Bright Star. All three of you are at the height of your power. It is the hope of the Senior Council of Bright Star that you will successfully defend our Fair and restore Moonrise."

Judge Rogers laid his hands on Kirsten's head. "Kirsten. You are the Connector of this Knot. Your skills have always been in bringing people together. I now empower you to be this new Knot's Connector." Bright *bronze* light flared, leaving Kirsten glowing.

He bypassed Yesenia and stood in front of Shadow, setting his hands on her head. "Shadow, she who has lost her name. You have always had the strength to drive others to higher achievement. You are the Motivator of this Knot. I now empower you to be this new Knot's Motivator."

Iron blazed bright, briefly covering Shadow as Yesenia gasped, realizing what position was left.

But—that means—me? The Knot's Guide? The leader?

Me?

Judge Rogers smiled at her. "Don't look so scared, Yesenia. You have always possessed a clear vision, with definite goals.

You are the Guide of this Knot. I now empower you to be this Knot's Guide."

Copper burned through Yesenia, temporarily blinding her. She blinked and her vision came clear.

"Put your hands together," Commissioner Rogers said, as he came forward. He and Judge Rogers held their hands over Yesenia, Shadow, and Kirsten's joined ones.

"By the power vested in us by the Bright Star Senior Council, we tie the three of you together as Connector, Motivator, and Guide, to be Bright Star's Solo Knot," Judge Rogers intoned. "We command you to do these things to complete your position and become fully Solo. First. Discover who carries the aspects of Pale Wraith and Red Horseman in Bright Star, and neutralize them. Second. Defend Bright Star Fair from the Destroying Knot. Third. Discover what twisted witch holds the Moonrise Fair daemon hostage, and free that daemon from its captivity. Do the three of you accept this commission?"

"Yes," they chorused in unison.

"Then so be it, Yesenia, Shadow, and Kirsten. Go forward with the blessing of the Bright Star Senior Council—and good luck."

Judge Rogers exhaled, and seemed to shrink, becoming Wallace Rogers, Kirsten's father, once more, as did Commissioner—now Frederick—Rogers.

"Janna says that dinner will be ready in fifteen minutes." Wallace shook his head. "Extraordinary times. I would have wished to spare you—*all* of you, but that is not possible. Yesenia, Shadow, welcome to the protection of my household. You may remain here until such time as you are ready to safely establish your own homes."

Both he and Frederick bowed to each of the women, then left.

Kirsten was the first to speak. "Wow. This is—wow."

"This really changes things. Either all three of us will become Solo, or none of us will," Yesenia said. "My Great-Aunt Eufalia was once part of a Solo Knot. It's how she managed to save the Ocean Breeze Fair when it became Lost."

Shadow sniffled. "My Fair isn't completely Lost. I—what does that mean for my future? Will I need to return to my old Fair's territory once I become Solo, or am I permanently part of Bright Star?"

"My understanding, from what Eufalia said, is that participants in a Knot become even more independent than the typical Solo witch." Yesenia chewed her lip. Then she got up and dug in her spell bag. Part of Great-Aunt Eufalia's death-gift had been an annotated guide her great-aunt had kept during her early years as a Solo practitioner.

I hope I didn't leave it at the house.

Who knew what the Pale Wraith's presence could do to Yesenia's possessions? Yes, she had always secured her personal journals and witch-related items—a matter of safety when there were children with witch potential in the household. But would her wards stand up to the Pale Wraith?

Yesenia's daemon stirred, guiding her fingers through spells and guides, until she touched a well-worn, cloth-over-cardboard book cover.

Aha.

Her fingers knew the guidebook better than her eyes. She extracted it.

"What's that?" Kirsten asked.

"*The Handbook for Newly Solo Witches.* It belonged to Eufalia, and she passed it to me as part of her death-gift."

"What does that do to help us?" Kirsten squinted at the elaborately curlicued title and well-worn cover edges. "I mean, that's an *old* book. Will it work for modern witchcraft?"

"Eufalia kept notes in it. I haven't read it much," Yesenia said. "She warned me not to open it very often until I had need, because it could lead me down the twisted paths if I wasn't ready. I *hope* that she recorded information about forming her Solo Knot, and what they did to save Ocean Breeze Fair."

"Ohh," Shadow whispered reverently. "I've heard about this version of the *Handbook*. My mentor—may the Mother of Magic have kept her safe during the chaos—had one." She blinked. "But her copy was lost, along with the Fair."

Yesenia set the book down on the cutting table.

"So where is the section about Knots and saving Fairs?" Kirsten started to reach for the *Handbook*, but Yesenia pushed her hand away as her daemon screeched in warning.

"Wait! You don't just open this book. It's only attuned to me, and I have to be careful when I open it."

"It has the original spellcasts?" Shadow asked.

"I think so."

"Just how do we access it if we don't touch it?" Kirsten grumbled.

"Like this." Yesenia held her hands over the book. "Um. I think, since we're a Knot, that we need to do this together. But I don't know how to do that!"

Shadow swallowed hard. "I think I do. We need to put our hands on your shoulders, and you ask for what you need to know."

Kirsten cocked her head. "It's worth a try."

"So what do we ask?" Yesenia took a deep breath. "I don't know much about the Pale Wraith and the Red Horseman."

"I know just enough about the Red Horseman to get into trouble," Shadow whispered. "I'd like to find an easier way to counter him."

"And if the Pale Wraith has control of my family, I need to know how to deal with her," Yesenia said.

"Let's ask the book how the Solo Knots defend the Fairs against those entities," Kirsten said slowly. "Not quite those words. Let your daemon guide you, Yesenia."

Yesenia nodded. She waited until their hands were on her shoulders. Then she summoned her daemon, pausing until *copper* filled her mouth, pushing the daemon's power into her hands.

"Find. How do Solo Knots defend a Fair when it is challenged by the Pale Wraith and the Red Horseman?"

A light glowed over the book, and it opened. Yesenia pulled her hands back as a likeness of Great-Aunt Eufalia appeared above it—not Eufalia herself, but a daemon in her likeness. This hadn't happened when she glanced through the book before!

"Ah, Yesenia, my girl. I see you are part of a newly-made Knot. So the Red Horseman and the Pale Wraith challenge the Bright Star Fair?"

Yesenia's mouth felt dry and full of cotton as she stared at Eufalia's image. She coughed before speaking. "The Pale Wraith claimed the Cruz family matrix this morning. The Senior Council has advised us that both it and the Red Horseman seek to bring down the Bright Star Fair."

"Your Motivator bears the mark of someone who barely escaped the Red Horseman. And you, girl, have been brushed by the Pale Wraith. That is certainly evidence of the threat. Both of you are more vulnerable to those entities."

"So what must we do to defend Bright Star against the Horseman and the Wraith?"

"First, you must identify the witches who currently bear the Wraith and the Horseman. Do you know who they are, yet?"

"No idea who carries the Horseman," Yesenia said slowly. "But this morning—it was Marisol who appeared to bear the Wraith."

"Ah, Marisol, Marisol. Of course it would be her."

"Papa was calling in an exorcist."

"That will not be effective until you—not an outsider—have defeated the Wraith. Hm. I wonder what variant of the Wraith this is?"

"Variant?" Yesenia hadn't heard that the Wraith—or the Horseman, for that matter—came in different forms.

"Yes. Join your strengths in the Knot now and extend your awareness. Spy on the family matrix—don't get caught!—and identify the following elements: what does the Wraith's magic taste like, what does

it smell like, and how does it feel? That will tell you what you need to know."

"How does it feel?" Yesenia frowned, confused. "What do you mean by that?"

"Texture. Sensation. Greasy, oily, wet, scratchy, gritty—you need those three elements to understand what you are up against. The same will be true of the Horseman—what you learn about the Wraith's magic will help with the Horseman. You must know these three things to battle them safely. Get this information as soon as possible, then ask me again."

The book slammed shut, and the daemon that resembled Eufalia disappeared with a *pop!*

"Well," Shadow sighed. "I certainly could have used *this* knowledge when I was fighting the Red Horseman. Do we wait, or shall we try now?"

"If we wait, I'll have time to fret about it," Yesenia said. "Let's do it."

Kirsten pulled a chair over from the sewing machine setup and placed it in front of the couch. "I wish our seniors would tell us more about how Knots really work. It's like we're just being tossed out there to sink or swim."

"My mentor once said that each Knot needs to find its own way of working," Shadow said, settling on the couch.

"Trial and error, I guess. Like a lot of magic. I mean, learning how to manage your Fair daemon doesn't exactly come with a lot of guidance. Even from all those handbooks." Yesenia sat next to Shadow. "Certainly not how to win it in the first place. It seems to be all about what works for each witch. I suppose the Knot is the same way."

Kirsten frowned as she sat in the chair. "I don't think that shoulder touch is enough. Especially if we're going against the Pale Wraith. Put your knees around mine, both of you, and let's hold hands. Then you can raise the Knot, Yesenia. I mean— Shadow, this is what has worked best for me and Yesenia when we're doing a working together. I suppose that would be the same thing for you as well."

"All right."

They arranged themselves, then held hands. Yesenia closed her eyes, calling up her daemon. *Copper* rose.

There had to be an order to their linkage. Who should she connect to first—Kirsten, the Connector, or Shadow, the Motivator?

You need the Connector to make the Motivator work, she decided. Then she reached out for Kirsten's *bronze* magic. *Copper* and *bronze* twined around each other, but there was a gap in the flow.

A space for Shadow.

That turned out to be correct when she reached for Shadow's magic. *Iron* inserted itself into the gaps, making a unified whole of their three daemons.

Yesenia inhaled. Then she thought about *home.*

Three seconds, and they were *there.*

At first, everything seemed to be regular. Normal. No change from what the family and the matrix had been yesterday.

Then a cool, cloying sensation brushed across Yesenia's face. She gasped as it began to sting.

Marisol darted into the living room. "What are *you* doing here? Begone!" She pointed the index and ring fingers of both hands at Yesenia. Saul sauntered in behind Marisol and put his arms around her. The two of them shimmered, and that cool, sticky feeling grew thicker, with little needle-like prickles stinging Yesenia's face.

Something tugged at her. Yesenia pushed back, but it kept pulling, pulling, pulling at her.

Then *bronze* and *iron* flared around Yesenia.

They were back in Kirsten's basement. Yesenia gasped for breath.

"We failed," she moaned. "*We failed.* Marisol saw me and—and—" No. She couldn't share that last piece with Saul, not unless the others saw it too.

"Did either of you feel anything?" Shadow asked. "Because I kept tasting something that was smoky and burnt."

"I didn't taste anything," Kirsten said, scrunching up her face. "But oh did your house ever reek of spoiled fish, Yesenia!"

"Then we didn't fail. All three of us gathered a piece of the information we were asked to find." Yesenia made herself breathe slowly, evenly. "I had a cool, sticky sensation that thickened on my face and started to sting."

Shadow shook her head and frowned. "How does it all fit together?"

"Time to go back to the book," Kirsten said firmly. "The daemon told us to report back."

Yesenia slowly pushed herself upright. Mother of Magic, the last thing she wanted to do was more spellcasting. She was tired and needed food.

But—they had this to do, they needed to come up with the comic routine they had promised to the Bright Star Fair daemon before bed tonight—and tomorrow was a long day. Get this piece over with.

She mustered her strength and walked over to the cutting table.

This time, the daemon manifested itself quickly.

"You have the experiences? Good. Each of you think of them."

It touched Kirsten's forehead, then Shadow's, and finally Yesenia's.

"So?" Yesenia asked when the daemon retreated to the book.

It held up one finger. *"A moment. This is a very old mixture. A version of the Pale Wraith that has not risen for many years."* It phased through several shapes, Eufalia fading to a form akin to Marisol and Saul embracing that made Kirsten gasp, then taking on a different form that caused the same reaction from Shadow.

At last, it stabilized. *"Ladies. This will prove to be a difficult challenge for all three of you. Yesenia, you are very fortunate in your Knot partners, because you were almost captured. The Pale Wraith is definitely in Marisol's form. Should you see her on the Fair Grounds, immediately throw salt on her. That will not banish her, but will temporarily immobilize her."*

"Can one of us write these instructions down without breaking our Knot link?" Yesenia asked.

"Better yet, I will transcribe them. Second. The Red Horseman rides someone close to the Fair's management. I do not know who yet. They carry Moonrise, and have not yet fully consumed it."

"Then what happens when it is rescued? Do I need to go back to my Fair?" Shadow asked.

"No. As part of a Knot, you are beyond Fair area restrictions on your magic." The daemon waved its hands dismissively. *"We can deal with that later. Third. The three of you are much stronger together than apart. Temptations will try to break you apart from the Knot. If you yield, the Knot is destroyed, the Fair is Lost, and all three of you will fail. Be prepared!"*

The daemon disappeared. In its place, on top of the book, lay three small sheets of paper, with the daemon's instructions carefully scribed in a flowing red script.

"Dinner!" Janna called from upstairs, startling them.

"I suppose we should put these into our spell bags," Kirsten said. "And then, after dinner—the comic routine design and choreography?"

Yesenia wanted to do nothing more than curl up and rest.

But. That wasn't possible. Not yet.

She had work to do.

CHAPTER 6

THE FAIR CROWN'S WORK MUST BE APPROVED BY THE FAIR COMMITTEE

B efore the events of the Fair can begin, the Fair Committee must approve of the Fair Tapestry, the morning after the Tapestry Sing. The Committee must be made up of former witches and Typicals. No active witches may participate in the Tapestry approval, other than the Fair Crown, her Court, and their musicians.

The Fair Crown's Handbook, Ninth Edition

THE NEXT MORNING, YESENIA AND HER COURT ASSEMBLED IN THE Style tent, wearing their Sing outfits as they waited nervously for the Fair Committee's arrival. Approval of the Tapestry was the final step before the Fair officially opened to non-witches—and this was the first time the Committee would have been on site for this year's Fair.

Tobias and the musicians set up their instruments, their low murmurs echoing through the tent.

Yesenia tapped her fingers together, concerned about that animation spell that she had implanted into the Tapestry. It was a new technique that she had been wrestling with over the past year, and even with Eufalia's death-gift, it was difficult.

Are you ready? she asked Bright Star.

The daemon stirred. *I have had a lovely time tasting this Tapestry and sampling its pieces. It is an intricate construction.*

Will the animation work?

As long as there is no interference, Bright Star answered. *And may I congratulate you on your new status, as part of a Solo Knot. I am honored to be present at the birth of yet another Knot.*

Thank you.

A chime sounded from the wards.

"Beware! Typicals!" Tobias called. "The Fair Committee approaches!"

"Cloak your magics," Yesenia ordered her Court. "The drum!"

BOOM-boom! Tobias pounded on the big kettledrum. The faint buzz of active magics settled as the Court moved to each side of the Tapestry, leaving Yesenia alone in front of it.

Another drummer began a soft, muted rat-a-tat-tat march.

Yesenia quickly scanned around her, searching for any trace of active magic.

Nothing. Good.

She raised her hands. "Let the Fair Committee enter, and may the Tapestry receive its first judging," she pronounced in bold, ringing tones that carried throughout the enclosure. "Welcome the Committee, all witches!"

"Welcome the Committee!" the Court and musicians roared.

Their pride in this latest Tapestry filled Yesenia with unexpected joy. She wanted to throw her head back and laugh as the heady, intoxicating essence of their satisfaction with this Tapestry flowed through her.

And yet—there was one small, dissonant piece that cloaked itself before Yesenia could trace it.

Did you feel that? she asked the Fair daemon.

Very briefly, it answered. *I do not know who it was.*

No time to figure it out now. But it was someone *here*, which meant her Court, or her musicians…no time to puzzle through this further, as the spell dump daemon opened the tent door. The Fair Committee marched in.

Yesenia schooled her face into the acceptable submissive, pleasant expression that this Committee expected from its witches. Rosalee led the Committee, leaning heavily on her cane, smiling and nodding at the Court as she hobbled up the steps and down the runway to stand in front of the Tapestry.

The two men and three women that followed Rosalee were more stern-faced. Pauline Eddings, the Chair, pressed her lips together disapprovingly as she took her position on the other side of the Tapestry from Rosalee, her stiff white hair not wavering a strand. She averted her gaze from Yesenia as she walked by.

Was she a threat?

Unlikely. As Yesenia had learned over the past two years, Eddings's disapproval of witches was tied to her church background. She carried no real power—at least none capable of threatening any but the youngest witches still learning their first spells.

Now Oren Tillstrom, her Second—

Tillstrom simpered at Yesenia as he sidled by her on his way to stand next to Rosalee. He was a former witch who had given up his daemon at age twenty-one—rumor had it that he had tried and failed every means available to become Solo, and no family matrices found him skilled enough to be worth recruiting. Since he was that rarity, a witch from a non-witch family, his abilities needed to be stellar.

From what Yesenia had heard about Tillstrom, his skills would have just barely qualified him to participate in a family matrix, had he been born into a witch family. Without that family connection—well, there were plenty within witch families who needed to be provided for within a family matrix. If an outsider like Tillstrom brought no additional powers a matrix needed—there was no place for him.

Yesenia chewed her lip thoughtfully.

Could Tillstrom be a potential threat? He had a motive to be angry toward witchkind.

Tillstrom *had* been sealed against further daemon incursions —all the same, as he came close to Shadow, she startled, flinched, looked worried for a moment, then regained her pleasantly welcoming smile.

The next three Committee members were new this year, and clustered in a group as they approached the Tapestry and the Court. Yesenia paid extra attention to the expression and mood she projected with these three. Odds were that their only previous live magic exposures had come through watching Fair Competitions.

Tillstrom was the closest thing to a witch who would be allowed on the Committee. The others came from families lacking any sort of talent that would attract the land's daemons. That was a requirement for Committee membership. Tillstrom had squeezed in because his family had been amongst the original non-witch settlers who signed the Compromise that allowed Fair daemons to protect the witches within their domains.

Yesenia curtseyed to each of the new members. One wore an old steampunk signet ring, a relic from the era when Typicals had used mechanical technology to defeat witches. A dampening spell clung to it. Yesenia frowned.

Why is it dampened and not decommissioned?

All of those old rings were supposed to have been decommissioned. Clearly, this one hadn't.

And in the hands of a Committee member.

Threat, or not?

Is that ring a problem? she asked Bright Star.

The daemon yawned. *I can swat that one down in my sleep. Do not be troubled.*

The Committee finished moving to their places.

Yesenia took a deep breath. "Ladies and gentlemen of the Committee. I present this year's Fair Tapestry. I pray that it will meet with your approval, so that we may open the Fair."

She gestured toward the Tapestry.

Activate animation spell, she ordered.

Ripples washed over the Tapestry as a cornucopia of bright colors and patterns shifted from a portrait of the current-day Fair into a replication of a late-nineteenth-century Fair. A steam-powered tractor puffed along a track leading to one of the livestock barns, pulling a shavings wagon. The people working around the barns paused as their clothing shimmered, then changed from modern t-shirts and jeans to stiff dark canvas trousers with suspenders and high-necked white shirts for the men and boys, and long calico dresses, aprons, and bonnets or scarves for the women and girls. Then they went back to work.

One woman led a black Clydesdale mare with a prancing foal at her side.

Tillstrom pushed forward to squint at the Tapestry. He reached out, and Rosalee deftly blocked his hand with her cane.

"Remember, we don't touch the Tapestry," she reminded him.

"Harrumph," Tillstrom snorted. But he stepped back. "It looks like things are *moving* in that Tapestry. Is there something wrong with it? Has it been infested?" His voice rose, an eager note in it suggesting that he hoped this was true. If so, the Committee could reject this Tapestry, and then—Bright Star's magic would not be renewed at the Fair this year. Not quite *losing* the Fair, but close. The ability for witches to draw power would be restricted.

"No, no, no," Yesenia said quickly. Best not to let *that* rumor start. "It is only an animation spell, and I took a fancy to making it look like the old days, to fit this year's Fair theme of *Those Good Old Days.* That's all."

"What purpose does *that* serve?" Tillstrom grumbled.

"Well, if Kirsten or I are here, we can enlarge a section so that viewers can watch multiple events at the same time—as long as there isn't a competition on stage."

"Really?" One of the new Committee members—*not* the one with the ring—*Anitra Gribov,* Yesenia remembered, leaned forward. "Wow! Look at Marya's filly trot!" She pointed at the section with the black Clydesdale. "Can you make that scene bigger?"

Yesenia gestured toward Kirsten. "Kirsten, if you would—?"

Kirsten stepped forward. They had practiced this, but Yesenia still watched nervously as Kirsten began softly singing the cue phrase.

Not so cautious, not so delicate, if she doesn't start to master it—

The Tapestry bulged and threatened to strain at the section Kirsten was invoking, forming a big bubble instead of maintaining its normal thready texture. Kirsten's lips tightened and she paled, her voice wavering.

Not like that! Bright Star snapped.

I know! Yesenia growled. *But she has to learn how to do this.*

Something is interfering. Something is causing a problem, the Fair daemon continued to protest.

Out of the corner of her eye, Yesenia saw Shadow gesture, forming the *avert* sign. The bubble in the Tapestry stopped swelling. It pulsed, then expanded properly. Kirsten's voice steadied, until the image of the black Clydesdale mare and her foal stabilized. The filly trotted back to her dam, her brush of a tail raised high, eyes wide and bright at all the new-to-her things. The mare chuckled a reassuring, deep, whinny. The foal answered with a higher-pitched note, then thrust her nose under her dam's belly to nurse.

Laughter rippled through the Committee.

"Now that's a good one!" chuckled Dawn McKenzie, another of the new Committee members.

But Tom Kendall, the new member who wore *that ring,* frowned. "Isn't this an overly ambitious magical working? It almost looked like Kirsten lost control of it."

"It is the first attempt we made toward animating the Tapestry since it was born," Yesenia said smoothly, before anyone else could respond. "A new Tapestry needs practice. I promise, by the end of Fair today, we will be seeing multiple animations without any glitches."

Yesenia vowed that if *a new Tapestry needs practice* wasn't already in any of the multiple Fair Crown and Tapestry management handbooks out there, then she would make good and sure that it was included in the next releases. It had been true for previous Tapestries.

Kendall's lips tightened. He glanced over at Tillstrom. The two men exchanged nods.

"*I* think that our Fair Crown has done a marvelous job this year." Rosalee raised her chin defiantly, glaring at the other Fair Committee members.

Eddings raised a magic detector. She walked back and forth in front of the Tapestry, her gaze fixed on it. Finally, she stopped in front of Yesenia.

"Congratulations, Fair Crown," she said. "Despite that—almost-outbreak of uncontrolled magic—none of the energies escaped your Tapestry. Nor did my detector go off during that flare." She turned to the others. "I move that this Tapestry is acceptable, and that we certify its control over the magic entities at this year's Bright Star Fair. Are there any objections?"

Silence. Eddings eyed each Committee member.

"Hearing no objections, I now certify this Fair."

BOOM-BOOM-BOOM-BOOM.

Tobias pounded the big kettledrums over and over, augmenting the beats until they echoed beyond the Style tent.

Eddings bowed to the Court, then raised her head and marched down the runway, followed by the Committee members. Rosalee winked at Yesenia.

"Group Style competition begins in an hour," she said.

"Court is dismissed," Yesenia said.

She started to leave, but Shadow gently grabbed her wrist, then Kirsten's.

"Wait for a moment."

They stood at the end of the runway, stepping aside to let the others leave.

When everyone except the musicians had left, Shadow bent in close to them.

"One of the Committee members is a betrayer. I sensed Moonrise. It called to me."

"Tillstrom?" Yesenia remembered how Shadow had flinched when he walked by her.

"I'm—not sure," Shadow said. "He startled me because I smelled magic on him. But he's not a witch!"

"He was one, until he renounced his daemon," Kirsten said.

Shadow tightened her lips, and shook her head. "I'm not sure if it is him or one of the others. Perhaps more than one. Perhaps not them, but someone close to them." She paused. "That *smoky, burnt* taste came into my mouth during your working, Kirsten. That's why I made the *avert* sign."

"I didn't feel anything," Yesenia said.

"Nor did I smell anything," Kirsten said thoughtfully. "But the spell became easier to control after you made that sign."

"I think we had better not be alone when we are working the Tapestry," Yesenia said.

"I agree," Shadow said. "Something is not right. We need to be watchful. I ignored my instincts the year my Fair became Lost. We dare not risk it happening to us."

Yesenia couldn't argue with that.

NORMALLY, ONCE THE TAPESTRY WAS APPROVED AND FAIR officially opened, Yesenia would plunge into the flurry of activities that surrounded the three-day Fair run. Group Style, with its overriding characteristic of humor. Regular Style, deadly serious in comparison because everyone's outfits were intended to display their potential Solo design skills. Judging of exhibits and seeing what ribbons she and her friends had won. The spell competitions that were a part of earning Fair Crown—though, with her successful Tapestry, unless something went really wrong, Yesenia was pretty much guaranteed that third Crown now.

Gorging on junk food from the Fair concession booths, for once not caring what she ate. Prowling through the livestock and horse barns, admiring the animals. Playing carnival games with Saul, both the magical and non-magical ones.

As Fair Crown it was Yesenia's duty to play and be seen. And since she was vying for her third Fair Crown, it was even more important that she have a Presence, and be publicly happy and celebratory.

Even if she didn't really feel like it, and wanted to search out who was carrying that Red Horseman. Even if she occasionally gulped and fought back tears at the memories of playing games with Saul. Now, more than ever, it was important that she follow through and at least *appear* to have fun.

Even if she was frightened, worried, and heartbroken about Saul's apparent defection.

Maybe she was imagining things. Maybe that truck had belonged to someone else. Maybe Maria had finally found herself a boyfriend.

Maybe.

But it was worrisome the way that Maria disappeared, not to be seen.

She was part of the Court. She needed to be *here*, not doing— whatever Maria was doing, out of sight, away from the Fair.

THE COMIC ACT THAT KIRSTEN DEVISED FOR THEM WAS BASED ON Bright Star's history. The first settlers in Bright Star had been witches and exiled daemons fleeing persecution in the East and Midwest. Their native counterparts welcomed the exiles, witchkind and daemons alike. When the missionaries and early steam mechanics arrived, attempting to complete their exorcism of North America, the groups banded together to battle the intruders.

A difficult time.

And yet, as Bright Star itself had said, it had been an era where tricks and fun were more common. The witchkind and daemon victory had its foundation in a massive practical joke played on the missionaries and mechanics, defusing their attempts at exorcism and covering them with piles of buffalo dung. Casting the joke spell brought around the creation of the first Solo Knot, which provided witches and daemons with a means to unite in order to defeat their opponents.

Kirsten *swore* that having the appropriate costumes on hand and an already-written short skit about the formation of Bright Star's first Solo Knot was a coincidence.

Yesenia wasn't so sure about that.

A Knot's Connector often *visualized* the need for specific tools in advance, often without knowing why they were necessary. This wasn't the first time that Kirsten had devised the right spell, outfit, or skit for a situation, long before she knew it was necessary.

Kirsten was destined to become our Connector, then.

So what had Yesenia and Shadow done to earn their roles? Yesenia certainly didn't *feel* like she had done anything to earn the title of Guide. She could see Shadow as a Motivator. But what about her? Was Yesenia just the Guide by default?

She hid those feelings from both her personal daemon and the Fair daemon. Neither Bright Star nor her own daemon needed the distraction.

∾

THEY WON THE GROUP STYLE PRESENTATION, IN SPITE OF HAVING only a short practice last night, and then a second quick run through after the Committee approved the Tapestry.

"I don't believe it!" Shadow exclaimed as they returned to the Tapestry after they had changed out of their costumes. "We won. Kirsten, that's one step toward you winning Style Crown."

"All in the power of the Knot." Kirsten smirked at Yesenia and Shadow.

"Harrumph!" Maria's snort startled them. "So what's with you, Yesenia and Kirsten? All of a sudden you're buddy-buddy with this *outsider*." She gestured at Shadow.

So now she shows up?

"Witches are supposed to give sanctuary to other witches who have lost their Fairs," Yesenia said, her all-too-brief cheerful mood flitting away. "You know that, Maria!"

"Doesn't mean you have to prioritize them over your other friends."

"Maybe friends shouldn't be running off with other friends' fiancés, either." Yesenia clenched her fists, scowling at Maria. "Then maybe they would have been included in the planning."

"What are you saying?" Maria wheeled to face Yesenia, her fists also tightening.

"You heard me. I saw Saul driving through the parking lot, picking you up yesterday after the Sing!"

"You're mistaken." But Maria's face paled.

"May have been traveling under a glamour, but I know the sound of Saul's truck anywhere!"

"Not supposed to drive with a glamour—" Maria countered.

"Saul's had to use a glamour recently because of problems with his truck! Stop lying to me, Maria." Yesenia dropped her voice until it was barely above a whisper. Rage flooded through her, and suddenly Maria appeared to be the *perfect focus* for it. Right there. Handy. Convenient. An appropriate outlet.

Yesenia charged toward Maria. Shadow and Kirsten grabbed her arms and wrenched her to a stop just several strides away from Maria. Yesenia struggled against their grip, but couldn't break free.

"Get *out* of here, Maria, and stop agitating Yeni," Kirsten snarled. "I heard Saul's truck last night too. Didn't see it. Didn't want to upset Yeni, but if she already knows—"

"*Betrayer*," Shadow hissed, wrestling with Yesenia. "There was one just like you at my Lost Fair! Are you with the Destroyers or not?"

Maria backed away from them. "You haven't won Style for certain yet, Kirsten! Neither have you earned that last Fair Crown, Yesenia! Just you wait!" She ran out the door.

Yesenia growled and broke free from Kirsten and Shadow. She chased after Maria until Shadow grabbed her arm.

"Let me go!" Yesenia tried to yank free.

"No! Don't you realize—she's baiting you!"

"How do you know that?" Another jerk.

Shadow grabbed Yesenia's other arm and pulled her around, so that they were facing each other. "Because I fell for the same thing at my Fair! Maria's been touched by the Horseman. She's being used."

Yesenia stopped struggling. She stared at Shadow. "You're sure?"

Shadow nodded.

DANGER! Bright Star shrilled, its cry picked up by Yesenia's daemon. *DANGER-DANGER-DANGER-DANGER.*

What's wrong?

Yesenia and Shadow turned toward the Style tent. Wavering, colorful lines pulsated in front of it, blurring the outline of what should have been an open door.

"Attack on the Tapestry!" Shadow shouted.

Yesenia sprinted off. Shadow caught up with her in two strides—but where was Kirsten? She had stayed behind—*oh no, we left her alone to guard the Tapestry*—

Yesenia groaned.

Bubble.

That was what blocked the Style tent door. Hopefully one cast by Kirsten—Yesenia slid to a stop.

"*No,*" she wailed.

The bubble surrounded Kirsten, who lay on her side in front of the Style tent, eyes closed. Marisol bent over Kirsten's collapsed body. As Yesenia and Shadow hurried toward them, the form of the Pale Wraith shimmered over both Kirsten and Marisol.

Then Marisol disappeared, along with the bubble.

"Kirsten!" Yesenia screamed, dropping to her knees by her friend's body. "*Kirsten!*"

Shadow knelt beside Yesenia as others started to crowd in around them. She gently touched Kirsten's neck, then turned a wide-eyed, frightened gaze toward Yesenia.

"*Oh no,*" she whispered. "Wraith curse. Mother of Magic. This is just like what happened at my Fair. The Pale Wraith has cursed her. Yesenia, now what? How can the Knot succeed without our Connector?"

Yesenia clenched her hands and bit her lip to keep from crying. Rage flooded through her. It wasn't fair! This just wasn't fair! There had to be a way to keep their opponents—whoever they really were—from destroying Bright Star.

"I'll make them pay," she muttered. "There has to be a spell that counters this. And then we're going to *find* the carrier of the Red Horseman and curse them. Curse Marisol. Are you with me?"

"We need to help Kirsten first," Shadow said, her voice trembling.

"How?"

"You witches aren't as powerful as you thought, heh?" Oren Tillstrom's voice rose above those of the others crowding around them.

Yesenia's head jerked up. She scanned the people staring at them—and Kirsten's limp body. Tillstrom's sneaky, sneering face wasn't amongst those watching.

Projection.

She scrambled to her feet, half-noticing that Anitra Gribov and Rosalee were herding the crowd away, murmuring that the witches needed to be left alone to deal with this issue.

"Where are you going?" Shadow asked.

"I'm going to find that—that destroyer!"

"What destroyer? Yesenia, we need to help Kirsten."

"You didn't hear him sneering at us?" Yesenia glared down at Shadow.

Shadow shook her head. "Yesenia. The Red Horseman has already distracted you once, and brought us to this situation. We have to help Kirsten."

"Tillstrom's carrying the Red Horseman. I *know* it. That's the only way that Marisol could have managed a projection—either that or she's stolen control of the family matrix from Mama!" Yesenia shuddered.

Shadow took her hands. "And the Horseman is enticing you. *Listen* to me. If Maria hadn't lured you away and I hadn't followed, Kirsten wouldn't have been here alone." Her grip tightened. "Listen to me. *Think.* I don't know you all that well yet, but what I *do* know is that you don't usually act like this. We have to help Kirsten." She blinked. "*Calm.*"

Yesenia gulped as Shadow's daemon pressed against her, projecting *calm*. She drew a deep, shuddering breath as it soothed both her and her daemon.

Shadow nodded as Yesenia blinked, then relaxed. "Good. I didn't have anyone to do this for me at—" her lips tightened and she looked down, blinking hard. Then she raised her head. "Moonrise. I went chasing after vengeance, and in the process, I let my Tapestry die." A defiant tone came into her voice. "I let the Horseman and the Wraith distract me. I won't let it happen again! Not if I can help it!"

"But if we don't stop that destroyer, how do we save Bright Star and get Moonrise back? What about Kirsten?"

"We can't do it through vengeance. We have to focus on helping Kirsten. We need a complete Knot."

"Take her to the Tapestry." Tobias stood in the doorway. "It warned us and I was able to raise some protections, but Kirsten took the full brunt of the Wraith's attack. That's the first thing we can do for Kirsten."

Yesenia nodded, biting her lip.

Kirsten was *so still.*

~

WITH TOBIAS'S HELP, SHADOW AND YESENIA MANAGED TO CARRY Kirsten and lay her in front of the Tapestry.

Then Yesenia studied the Tapestry. As she feared, a gray spot blotted out the Style tent.

What is that? she asked Bright Star.

A reflection of the attempt to destroy me.

Was it her imagination or did Bright Star sound weaker?

"Shadow. We have to stop this infestation of the Tapestry."

"This is how it starts," Shadow said, staring at the Tapestry. "Just like this." She choked. "Even the Knot isn't enough. That gray area will spread, and—"

"We need a replacement for Kirsten—two of us won't be enough. But who?" Yesenia looked around. At the moment it was just them and the musicians in the tent.

She kept coming back to Tobias. He had returned to his kettledrums and stood over them, face buried in his hands.

Are he and Kirsten a couple?

No, that was silly. Mother of Magic, he was twenty years older than they were! And Tobias had taken a vow of celibacy to dedicate himself to his music. But Tobias and Kirsten had been friends, and Tobias knew things, especially about defenses—

"Tobias." She kept her voice low.

He raised his head, rubbing his face. "Yes, Fair Crown?"

"We need you to help our Knot mend the Tapestry. Come here."

Tobias approached them slowly, his footfalls reluctant and slow. "I'm no Crown."

"But you have been the lead Fair musician ever since you went Solo. You've been Kirsten's friend. You know a lot more about the Fair than I do. The Tapestry has been damaged. Shadow and I need a third." Yesenia took a deep breath. This was risky, this was going way out there in theory, but—

"Oh. *Oh,*" Shadow whispered. "I see it, Yesenia." She extended her hands to Tobias. "Come join our Knot. I am the Motivator. Yesenia the Guide. Kirsten is—our Connector."

"I don't have Kirsten's abilities." Tobias stopped short of them. "I'm a musician, nothing more."

"A musician who sees clearly," Yesenia said. "You visualize things, and make them happen. Just like Kirsten does with her creations. A Knot can have more than one Connector. And you are already Solo-certified. That gives us more strength."

"I don't have Kirsten's Connector skills!" Tobias glanced down at Kirsten, then back up. "But the Wraith—"

"And who kept the Wraith from entering the tent after it vanquished Kirsten?" The more Yesenia thought about it, the more it *fit.* "Toby, we *have* to fix the Tapestry. I don't know if that will heal Kirsten, but if the Tapestry's strength is sapped by—" She gestured toward the gray spot, then gasped.

It was growing.

Tobias jerked as he stared at the Tapestry. "Are you sure?"

"Toby, you're always in the tent." If Tobias didn't think he could be another Connector, what role could he fulfill in a Knot —oh. Realization swept over Yesenia. "You're always here to guard your instruments and watch over us. You're older. You know things we don't. You're our Guardian."

"No time to certify me—" But Tobias's gaze didn't move from the Tapestry.

"We should be able to do it ourselves—Yesenia, you're the

Guide." Shadow's words tumbled out, faster and faster as she spoke. "We have to take this chance. We don't have much of a choice. We have to stop this and save Moonrise!"

She speaks true, Bright Star said. *Tobias. I call you to my cause. Join the Bright Star Solo Knot. You are the fourth they need.*

Tobias shuddered. *I hear you, Fair daemon.*

Acknowledging that he heard the Fair daemon meant that he was worthy.

Realization slowly came across Tobias's face, his eyes widening. A brief flash of joy—Bright Star must have spoken to him alone. A slow smile brightened his expression.

"All right, then."

The three of them knelt next to Kirsten, Shadow taking one of her hands, Tobias the other, Yesenia taking Tobias and Shadow's hands. Their *copper* and *iron* magics flared. Tobias glowed with *steel*—how had she not realized that he was *steel*?

So how do we do this? Yesenia asked. *Bright Star, what must happen next?*

The Knot's core has been formed. Speak the words binding him to the Knot. The rest will come.

Yesenia bit back a grumble at hearing yet again that *the rest will come*. She was so sick of *"the rest will come."* At some point, couldn't witchkind find a better way to train the younger members, besides platitudes and dusty old handbooks that left out important information?

She shoved those thoughts aside. No time for that. Something she could deal with later—*when* Bright Star was safe, and she had become Solo.

Yesenia took a deep breath, recalling what Judge Rogers had said while forming their Knot. She didn't have the ability to *empower* their Knot's members, but perhaps she could invite Tobias. Confirm his presence. That sounded right.

Besides, unlike the three of them, Tobias was already Solo. He didn't need to prove his status.

"As the Guide of the Bright Star Solo Knot, I invite and

confirm Tobias as our Defender," she said. "Tobias has always guarded and protected the Style tent, the musical instruments, and the integrity of our Tapestries. He is worthy to be a part of the Knot."

Now what? Nothing tingled in her hands. What else needed to be done? Had she said the right words?

"As the Motivator of the Bright Star Solo Knot, I invite and confirm Tobias as our Defender," Shadow said.

Ah. Now Yesenia felt the faint stirring of power. So it wasn't something she could do by herself. But how to include Kirsten—*they* had to speak for her. She looked at Shadow. They nodded to each other. No need to speak confirmation—that would wreck the spell. If Yesenia led—she had to trust that Shadow would follow.

"In the name of our Connector, who cannot speak for herself and needs defense and protection, we invite and confirm Tobias as our Defender," she and Shadow said together, Shadow's voice lagging just slightly behind Yesenia's.

The visualization of *copper, iron,* and *bronze* twined together in a single cord suddenly appeared, shimmering over Kirsten's still form. *Steel* hovered nearby, tentative.

Make room for steel, she commanded.

An opening formed between *bronze* and *copper.* Yesenia reached out for *steel.* It glided into place with the barest of touches.

Just like that, Tobias was part of their Knot.

Yesenia thought about the space that was supposed to be the Style tent in the Tapestry. Together, *they* reached into the stuff that made up the Tapestry. *Steel* flowed into the eroded remains of *bronze* throughout the Tapestry, reinforcing and strengthening it. Once *steel* was settled, Yesenia concentrated on the original image of the Style tent. Try as she would, it kept shifting to something different.

Bright Star, help me!

It has changed, the Fair daemon said. *Do not fight it.*

Yesenia let the change in the working happen. The tent transformed from plain white to a mix of *copper, iron, bronze,* and *steel* threads, all intertwining, glowing brightly, flowing over the tent until it shimmered with the mixture of those threads. A virtual representation of their Knot's shielding of the tent.

Yesenia inhaled. Exhaled.

Activate.

The power flowed from them, then faded. Kirsten moaned, then turned to her side, blinking.

"What happened?" she whispered.

"The Pale Wraith," Yesenia said. "You defended the tent until the Wraith defeated you. I chased after Maria, and Shadow followed to stop me. Tobias kept it from coming inside. He's now part of our Knot."

"I *know* that part," Kirsten said, an irritable note in her voice. "I can feel his presence in the Knot." She rolled onto her back and rubbed her face, wrinkling her nose as she dropped her hands. "I can still smell the stench of spoiled fish. It happened too quickly to call either one of you—I didn't smell the Wraith until it was too late."

"Now that we are four, we need to stay in pairs," Yesenia said. "And we need to find out who the Red Horseman is."

"Oh, I know now," Kirsten said. "I wasn't *totally* helpless against the Wraith." She exhaled. "Oren Tillstrom is the Guide of a False Knot—and he's the Red Horseman. The only reason he is able to hide it from us is because he holds the Moonrise Fair daemon hostage. Moonrise covers his tracks."

Shadow bared her teeth. "I'll make him pay—"

"No," Tobias said, his voice carrying a strength and fullness it hadn't before. "Vengeance isn't the path. You said it right to Yesenia when dispelling the Horseman's lure. Vengeance distracted her and gave the Pale Wraith an opening to attack us. You are particularly vulnerable to the Red Horseman, Shadow."

Shadow swallowed hard. "You're right," she said in a low

voice. "But the thought of Moonrise in that—that false witch's clutches—"

"You can't think about that." Kirsten sat up slowly. "I saw a pattern while I wandered lost. A—Connector vision. We must find a means to attract the False Knot here, in full strength, and engage them."

Yesenia frowned. "How can we battle them safely? There are too many non-witches around us."

"They'll have a plan," Shadow said. "We can't just lure them here. They need the power of a special event. But which one?"

"Where would they be most likely to turn up? Yesenia, maybe it's time to bring out the *Handbook* again," Kirsten said.

"If I were planning an attack, it would be on the Tapestry," Tobias said slowly, thoughtfully. "And it would be tomorrow night, after Style Crown has been chosen, either before Fair Crown is chosen or right after. Strike at our moment of highest celebration."

"Do you agree?" Yesenia turned to Kirsten, then Shadow.

"The attack happened sooner for us—but we didn't have a Knot," Shadow said. "Given what we've gone through so far, and Bright Star's status—that makes a lot of sense."

"I agree," Kirsten said. She pursed her lips. "I don't think we should go home tonight. I'll call Mom and have her bring pillows and sleeping bags. We need to stay with the Tapestry."

Yesenia nodded. She looked back at the Tapestry. The new Style tent shimmered brighter than ever.

I will do whatever it takes to keep you safe, she vowed.

CHAPTER 7
UNITY IS THE KEY TO A WITCH'S POWER

T*he value of a family matrix or a Solo Knot is the unified power of witches working together. A witch by themselves is only as good as their individual skill. Witches joined together are more powerful than the sum of their abilities, whether their goal is creative or destructive. The history of Bright Star Fair has shown this truth, over and over again.*

A Witch's History of the Bright Star Magic Fair

TWENTY-FOUR HOURS TO WAIT IN THE TENT, GUARDING THE Tapestry.

Twenty-four hours until that final confrontation.

Maybe. Yesenia wasn't certain that their opponents would wait that long. Toby's arguments made sense, and yet—

Shadow was edgy and jumpy, as well. Memories from Moonrise?

It was just too easy that their opponents would wait until the awarding of both Style Crown and Fair Crown. Bright Star witches would all be present, at their highest and strongest moment of power. Wouldn't it make more sense to attack an apparently undefended Tapestry the night before?

But even as she worried, appearances had to be maintained. Yesenia and Kirsten took turns wandering around the Fair, pretending to play and be happy. Shadow went with whoever was out, while Tobias stayed behind in the tent.

Janna Rogers brought their supplies in early evening. "I don't know where you girls are going to sleep on site. Fair sweep at the end of the day is pretty comprehensive."

Kirsten had explained their rationale for pillows, sleeping bags, and personal supplies when she called her mother.

Tobias raised a brow. "The Fair security doesn't sweep everywhere. I've stayed on site for years."

Janna opened her mouth to speak, then shut it abruptly as she *looked* at Tobias.

"Knot Guardian. All right, then, I *should* trust you."

A quick smile brushed across Tobias's lips. "It seems that I have been a Guardian for longer than any of us have realized."

THEY GATHERED BY THE INSTRUMENT STAGE—TOBIAS HAD ALREADY moved the instruments into the guarded changing area—when the first call for Fair Closing went out on the loudspeakers. Tobias traced a circle on the tent wall. A bubble extruded from it.

"Grab your stuff and step inside." He tugged at the bubble. "Need to make it big enough to fit."

The four of them clambered into the bubble, dragging sleeping bags and pillows. Tobias damped it once they were inside, so that they could see out but not be seen. With a gentle flick of his fingers, four cots appeared.

"Hopefully this isn't *too* big," he said. "It can be detected if someone with strong enough magic *looks* just right at it."

Shadow took his hand. "Let's reinforce the shielding. I think just the two of us can do that—don't need the whole Knot to do everything."

They held hands as the bubble became more opaque. Just in time—Tillstrom and Tom Kendall entered the tent.

"Those meddling girls are gone?" Tillstrom growled.

"They aren't in here." Kendall shrugged. *Orange* glowed around his ring—Yesenia didn't recognize the magic.

And it was most definitely not dampened, like it had been during the Fair Committee's approval of the Tapestry!

Is Tillstrom truly the Red Horseman? Or has it been Kendall all along?

"No one has reported them leaving. I don't trust them. They could be in hiding."

Yesenia bit her lip. They had overlooked the possibility that their exit could be monitored.

A familiar laugh as Marisol joined the other two. "Janna Rogers was here earlier, and the girls haven't been seen since she left. Knowing how cowardly Yesenia is, she and the others probably slinked out under Rogers's cover."

Shadow tensed as the fourth person entered, an emaciated, dark-skinned man. While his features were those of a young man, *his eyes* were wide and staring, as if he had undergone many horrors.

"Shawn isn't any better, either," he said. "All of those witches are cowards. Otherwise, they'd be with us." But his voice lacked conviction, and when Kendall turned toward him, he flinched.

Shawn. Shawn Jones. Shadow's name. *Now* Yesenia remembered it.

"Jerome looks awful," Shadow whispered. "The Horseman has not been kind to him."

"Your ex-boyfriend?" Yesenia asked.

Shadow nodded, her lips rolled tight. "But why do they need *two* Horsemen, if Tillstrom is the one at Bright Star? Or is Jerome no longer carrying the Horseman? I don't get that feel from him."

"Shh." Tobias strained toward the edge of the bubble. "Let's hear what they're saying."

"So," Tillstrom drawled. "Shall we raise the Knot? Finish this farce once and for all? With Bright Star gone, then we can raise a new form of magic." He smirked as Jerome shuddered. "What's the matter? Too cowardly to sacrifice yourself to the Horseman once and for all? There is a price to be paid."

"*No*," Shadow whispered. She closed her eyes tightly. "That's why I don't sense the Horseman around him."

"I will pay the price to gain immortality," Jerome said. He pulled off his shirt. "I am no coward." He marched onto the runway and toward the Tapestry. It flinched and tried to slither away as he lay down in front of it. "Bring it on!"

The other three followed, scowling at each other. They raised a bubble before stepping onto the stage, muffling their voices. But it was clear that they were arguing.

"Blood sacrifice," Tobias murmured. "*That's* their plan. Doesn't look like they're agreeing on how to do it."

"You know about this?" Yesenia stared at Tobias.

"It's something you learn about as you become stronger in Solo status," he said. "We can't let this happen." He drew a deep breath. "Because Jerome has carried the Horseman, even though he doesn't have the Horseman riding him now, he still has power that they can use. But they'll have to kill him to make the Sacrifice happen, and it doesn't look like any of them have the guts to follow through. Immortality is not guaranteed."

"Whatever we do, we'd better act before they get that False Knot going," Shadow said.

"Raise our powers, then do—what?" Kirsten asked. "We'll have to step out of the bubble to do anything. Just like they will."

Yesenia glanced at Tobias. He nodded, and she suddenly *knew* what to do, even as Shadow gasped.

"Moonrise! They have to force Moonrise to unite with Jerome —or me—before they strike."

"How do you know that?" Kirsten demanded.

Shadow glared back at her. "Because Moonrise just sent a message to me. It's weak. It's been resisting, but—it knows its Crown is near." She exhaled and straightened to her full height. "Just like Bright Star can talk to Yesenia through the bubble. Don't talk to it now—that will tip them off." She grabbed Yesenia's hand.

"This is the message," Shadow mindspoke.

Yesenia put aside any questions and *accepted.*

A wordless flow of knowledge poured over Yesenia from Shadow. The Moonrise Fair daemon had sent jerky, animated pictures to Shadow instead of speaking—a clear sign that its resources were faltering. Yesenia absorbed the information, and winced at the flow of emotions from the Moonrise daemon at the end.

It's being tortured.

And, just like that, she knew what needed to happen.

Must be what the Eufalia daemon meant when it said that answers will come as we need them.

Still don't like that. I feel like a mushroom in the dark.

"All right," she said. "Here's what we need to do. Once they stop arguing, they'll raise their False Knot. We have to raise ours first, then act physically. Beat them to Jerome." She drew a breath. "I forgot to throw salt on Marisol when she attacked Kirsten. I will throw salt on her this time—that will slow their Knot. Shadow. Go to Jerome. Get him away from the Tapestry. Kirsten. Connect with Bright Star. Work with it to pull Moonrise out of Tillstrom. Tobias. That ring Kendall wears. He's the Defender of their Knot. You need to neutralize him. We'll have to work quickly, strike before they can raise defenses."

"All at once?" Shadow asked.

"Yes. I wonder if quantity of salt will make a difference in how long Marisol is paralyzed?"

"Worth a try." Kirsten fumbled in her spell bag and handed a small leather bag to Yesenia. "I forgot about using salt, too."

Shadow gave Yesenia her salt. Yesenia put the three bags at her feet, then spread her arms wide. "Push in as close as you can to me to form the Knot. Heads together as well."

They moved in close, bodies as tight against each other as they could. Yesenia raised *copper. Iron, bronze,* and *steel* twined with it, forming an even greater whole. This time it formed a knot, rather than a strand.

Yesenia raised her head.

Now, she ordered. *Everyone knows their parts.*

A quick squeeze, then they broke apart. Yesenia picked up the salt bags.

Shadow ran to the stage, leaping on it and skidding over to Jerome. The bubble containing the False Knot broke apart. Kirsten grasped Tillstrom from behind, before he could charge toward the Tapestry. Shadow dragged an unresisting Jerome away from the Tapestry. Tobias wrestled Kendall off of the stage.

That left Yesenia to face Marisol.

Her memory stuttered. She was supposed to do something— but what? Something to do with the bags in her hand that held a crumbly substance—

Yesenia eased one bag open. The moment her right index fingertip brushed the crumbly, rough rock salt crystals, she knew what to do.

She pulled out a handful of the salt as the Pale Wraith extracted itself from Marisol and loomed over Yesenia. For a moment that cool, cloying sensation brushed over her face. Yesenia startled.

Why do I have salt in my hand?

Marisol lunged at Yesenia, grabbing her right hand clenched around the salt, trying to pry it open. Yesenia jerked. Some of the salt dribbled onto Marisol, and she froze in place, fingers entwined with Yesenia's.

The *stuff* on Yesenia's face began to *sting*. Yesenia extracted her fingers from Marisol's, shook out the rest of the bag into her right hand, and rubbed the remaining salt onto Marisol's arm. The Pale Wraith *howled.*

The *stinging* progressed to *burning.* Yesenia whimpered. Tobias turned toward her. Kendall broke away from him to charge toward Yesenia. Tobias grabbed Kendall and yanked him back.

Yesenia choked back the pain, even though the agony began to tighten her throat. Noise was a distraction they couldn't afford. She emptied the second bag of salt into her right hand. First, she brought it to her face. The *burning* eased. Yesenia rubbed the rest of it over her face. The Pale Wraith screeched, retreating to Marisol, who was now flexing her hands again.

Now what?

Salt didn't seem to freeze Marisol for very long, much less the Wraith. Something more had to happen, but what?

And then Yesenia's thoughts cleared. She had one more bag of salt—

Running away won't help. Embrace your challenge.

Was that the faint trace of Bright Star in that thought?

No time to debate this further.

Yesenia emptied this bag into her right hand, then poured some of the salt into her left hand. She stepped in close to Marisol as her aunt wrapped her arms around Yesenia.

She brought both hands up and slapped them on Marisol's face. Not rubbing, just holding the coarse grains hard against Marisol's cheeks.

Marisol shrieked. Her brown eyes widened, pupils dilating.

Privileged little brat, always had the best of things, always thinking she's too good for the rest of us, what with her Fair Crowns and pretensions toward becoming Solo. Hanging out with that rich white girl Kirsten, getting notions above her station. I'll show her, and everyone else. I control the Pale Wraith. Eufalia's death-gift should have come to me, not her—

Marisol's thoughts circled back to *privileged little brat,* repeating themselves. She gasped as Yesenia pressed the salt harder against her skin.

"Did you not realize that the Pale Wraith always controls, and never is controlled?" Someone else spoke through Yesenia, in Spanish. "Marisol, my dear little one, why is it that you never seem to fully understand the implications of your choices? Why must you always behave as if you were the fool?"

"You—aren't—*her*!" Marisol's eyes widened even further, bigger than Yesenia thought was possible.

"I gave Yesenia my blessing for a reason." A sigh—also not from Yesenia.

Who is using me for their mouthpiece? Wait. Great-Aunt Eufalia?

Hush, child. No time to talk.

And then the *presence* glided from Yesenia and into her aunt. Marisol blinked, then collapsed.

Go now, child! Finish the battle. Bright Star needs you!

A delicate brush of fingers stroked Yesenia's cheek. It felt just like Great-Aunt Eufalia's fumbling reach to comfort Yesenia in the last weeks of Eufalia's life.

Then that gentle touch was followed by a *push*.

Yesenia whirled. Shadow had dragged Jerome to the edge of the stage and knelt on his chest, keeping him still, shouting encouragement to Kirsten as she vied with Tillstrom—not physical now, but the exchange of spectral energies that glowed bright *bronze* and tarnished *silver*.

Tobias had Kendall face-down on the ground, knees on his back, doing his best to wrench that ring off of Kendall's hand.

"Can you help me?" he yelled. "It won't budge."

Yesenia bolted toward him, jumping off the stage. A few salt crystals clung to her hands and she held them tight. Just in case. She dropped to her knees and grabbed Kendall's hand, grinding the crystals into it. He screamed and the ring glowed a brighter orange.

"Together," Tobias murmured. "Using the Knot."

But how—

Yesenia visualized the Knot. Was there a place where *copper* and *steel* twisted together?

Yes, and it was toward the bottom of the Knot manifestation, in a place where the combined threads of their magic twisted together. She eased *copper* and *steel* away from the others. Then she wrapped *herself* around that segment. The entwined strands glowed around her hand, then enclosed the ring.

It shattered.

A battered, frail daemon flitted out of the ring as Kendall sagged against the ground, no longer resisting Tobias. What remained of the daemon was gorgeous—royal blue, black, and silver shades wrapping around it.

"Moonrise!" Shadow called, longing echoing deep in her voice.

So it was Kendall and not Tillstrom who held Moonrise captive!

Kirsten and Tillstrom collapsed in a heap on the stage. Kirsten pushed herself up and away from Tillstrom as the daemon slowly made its way to Jerome and Shadow. Jerome stopped struggling as the Moonrise Fair daemon hovered next to them.

Oh my children, my children. Both so powerful, and yet unable to work together, the Fair daemon crooned, first stroking Shadow's cheek, then Jerome. *Both of you are broken.*

As are you, the Bright Star Fair daemon said, sliding out from its nest in the Tapestry. *It will take a full year or more for you to rebuild to the strength needed to restart your Fair.*

Is it worth it? The Moonrise Fair daemon studied Jerome and Shadow, shaking its head. *These two could have been the foundation for a powerful Knot. Like your just-born one, sibling. Instead, my Council and my Governors chose segregation by wealth and color. Not like yours.*

Sibling, things are not perfect here, either, Bright Star answered. *These*—it gestured to the fallen False Knot—*wanted to destroy me, just as they tried to do to you. But my children*—Bright Star preened slightly—*remembered to work together.* It paused. *And your child definitely helped keep them on track.*

But what shall I do? The one child betrayed me and is broken. The other—is now yours. Moonrise shook its head, then keened softly.

"Jerome has more potential to rebuild you than I do," Shadow said softly. She eased off of his chest. "I was greedy and selfish when I became Crown. I was afraid—and I lost it all."

Jerome pushed himself up slowly. "I didn't want to recognize your strength. I wanted you to serve me. I was wrong."

"I am now sworn to Bright Star. I am part of a Solo Knot. That future we dreamed of? Is gone." Shadow exhaled. She looked up at Moonrise. "I would love to be your rescuer, Moonrise. But—" she gestured toward Kirsten, Yesenia, and Tobias. "This is my Knot. This is my future. I was casual and careless about my bonds before. I will not be so again."

Jerome exhaled and buried his head in his hands. Moonrise rested itself on him.

Jerome. We are both shredded and broken. Perhaps we can build a future for Moonrise Fair, together.

He raised his head. "But will you be able to trust me?"

We both need healing. She has changed and will find her healing with Bright Star. You—will make it up to me by helping me rebuild a more equitable Fair. Do you choose this route?

Jerome shuddered. Exhaled.

"I do, oh Moonrise."

Then it will be so.

KIRSTEN CALLED HER FATHER WHILE SHADOW, JEROME, TOBIAS, AND Yesenia stood watch over the False Knot. Soon enough, not only the Council but the Fair Committee descended upon the Style tent.

"*Two* members of the Committee are Fair betrayers?" Pauline Eddings crossed her arms and glowered at Yesenia.

"Looks to be that way." Commissioner Rogers met Eddings's glare with one of his own.

"Bright Star confirms." Yesenia raised her chin and didn't flinch away when Eddings glared at her. "If you would like, I can raise it and let it speak to you through me."

Eddings shuddered. "No. That's fine. We don't need that to happen."

"Will we have enough members to appropriately vote on Style Crown and Fair Crown?" Anitra Gribov asked.

"We will," Rosalee said firmly, eying each Committee member firmly.

"Perhaps you young ladies should come home for the evening, now that the Tapestry is safe," Judge Rogers murmured.

Yesenia exchanged glances with Kirsten and Shadow. They nodded.

"We feel safer continuing to guard the Tapestry," she said. "While Tobias is an able Guardian, who knows what else may be out there? Our Knot will remain together."

"But *someone* needs to care for Jerome and Moonrise," Shadow added. "They need a space—preferably non-magical—to rest and begin their recovery."

"I can do that," Rosalee said. When the other Committee members stared at her, she shrugged. "What? I know how to handle witches in crisis. No magic around my house. I have no other family, and Moonrise will find it restful, as well as its host. The rest of you have families, some with young witches stirring."

"Thank you," Jerome said softly. He bowed low to Rosalee. "I will—*we* will—do our best to avoid becoming a burden upon you. Moonrise honors the administrator of Bright Star Fair."

Soon enough, the others left.

Tobias heaved a big sigh. "Do we want to remain in the bubble, or shall we pull our cots out?"

"I want to sleep by the Tapestry," Yesenia said firmly.

"We won't leave you alone," Shadow said, as Kirsten nodded.

The three of them ended up placing their cots next to the Tapestry, while Tobias set his in front of the doorway.

Yesenia dropped easily into sleep, lulled by the presence of Bright Star. The Fair daemon purred happily in her thoughts.

TOBIAS AND JEROME MET THE NEXT MORNING, BY THE MUSICIANS' stage. Yesenia couldn't hear what they were saying as she, Kirsten, and Shadow supervised the setup for the upcoming evening events.

"Yesenia." Her mother's voice spun Yesenia around. Her mother stood in the tent doorway. "So it is true about Marisol?"

"Yes."

Her mother shook her head sadly. "Poor Marisol. She wanted to win Fair Crown in her day, you know."

"Yes," Yesenia repeated. She gazed at her mother, suddenly just numb, not wanting to engage or say more.

Now that she was part of the Knot, there would be no going back to the Cruz family matrix. No other path but forward. No ties to anyone but the other Knot members.

At one point, the thought would have paralyzed her. Even as Solo, she would still have her family.

But this encounter made Yesenia realize what she was losing, as sorrow crossed her mother's face.

"We have lost two members of the family," her mother said. "Marisol—and you. And I do not know where we will find replacements. Oh, there are young witches coming up, but we are short on our experienced witches."

"Perhaps it is time for the Cruz family to look to witches not born into a family matrix," Yesenia said.

"We have not done that for almost a hundred years. Not

without marriage—and there aren't any family members available to marry outside witches now."

"Perhaps it is time for the Cruz family to do something different," Yesenia said. "I hear your concerns, Mother. As the Guide of the Bright Star Fair Solo Knot, I will consider them, and meditate on a solution."

Her mother's face tightened. Then she bowed low to Yesenia. "I hear the Guide's advice. Meditate well, she who once was my daughter."

Yesenia *should* have felt something as her mother walked away.

She didn't.

~

MARIA WAS SUBDUED AT THE STYLE COMPETITION, HER USUAL combative jibes quiet. After Kirsten was crowned, Maria pulled Yesenia aside.

"I have a confession to make, but I guess it's not so big a deal now that you're part of the Solo Knot." She kept her eyes averted from Yesenia's face.

"You and Saul." Yesenia kept her voice steady.

Now Maria dared to meet Yesenia's gaze. "I'm sorry. Saul was affected by the Pale Wraith and I—the Horseman."

Yesenia rested her hand on Maria's arm. "Make him happy, Maria. I never could." She paused. "Perhaps you should talk to my mother. The Cruz family matrix needs experienced witches, and I think you might fit in there."

Maria's eyes widened. "You're certain of that?"

"Talk to Saul. Talk to my mother. I know Saul has wanted to leave the Ramos matrix, and my mother already has approved him because of the relationship he and I had. I don't think that you will be a problem."

~

ONE OF THE CONSEQUENCES OF BECOMING PART OF THE SOLO KNOT was sharing the title of Fair Crown with her partners. Not that there were any questions about who would become Fair Crown this year—

As Guide, Yesenia was still the voice of the Fair daemon. Jerome managed to raise Moonrise in support.

And as the entire Fair joined in the final Sing, while Bright Star built the final montage that would represent this year's Fair and summarize the highlights, Yesenia blinked back tears when she saw the Fair daemon's creation.

The Knot—and Moonrise manifesting through Jerome— made up most of the print. The version of this year's Tapestry that would be preserved as long as the Bright Star Magic Fair endured.

"You'll be remembered forever." Kirsten jerked her head toward the center of the print, where Yesenia was represented as standing with outspread arms, *copper* radiating out from her fingertips.

"At least as long as Bright Star endures," Yesenia said.

"Well, that could be a while." Kirsten grinned. "And that, my friend, is well worth everything we've gone through."

Yesenia considered her friend's words. Then she leaned forward to study the Tapestry's print.

Do you see it? the Bright Star Fair daemon whispered to Yesenia. *Your possible future is there, if you choose it. You and I have one more year together, and then—this.*

Yesenia looked closer—there it was. A scene where she, Kirsten, and Shadow stood, arms entwined, gazing at their new boutique. Tobias stood to the side, looming over his drums, ready to start drumming. A shimmering *GRAND OPENING* banner hung on the storefront.

Is this real? Is it just this simple? she asked the Fair daemon.

It is a possible future, if you make it so. The path is never easy, but —if the three of you commit wholeheartedly to your dream, it will happen. You still have much to learn, and we have only one more year together.

Then you will guide us?

Yesenia suddenly was aware of the full, glowing power of the Fair daemon. *Witches must learn by doing, girl! All those handbooks and guides—they are but a pale shadow of the reality.* A soft, warm, caress of her cheek. *All this comes to nothing without the power of your Knot. Trust your Knot. Realize the power of togetherness. Learn your partners, and build your power as one. That is the true strength of becoming Solo.*

Yesenia bowed her head, smiling. *Then becoming Solo is not a path to take alone?*

It never has been. Now. Go forth and enjoy, with your friends! I look forward to what you and your Knot can achieve!

"Yeni," Kirsten whispered, as they dismissed the other witches. "The Solo sigil. It's glowing bright over you. But I've never seen one like it before. It's—all four of our daemons."

Yesenia looked at her friend, her eyes widening at what she saw. "A Knot, with *copper, iron, bronze,* and *steel* entwined?"

"Yes, but—"

Yesenia pointed to Shadow. The same knot-shaped sigil glowed over her as well. And Tobias—*yes.*

Tobias laughed. "Welcome to becoming Solo! Congratulations!" He opened his arms wide. "And we are a Knot of Solos."

The four of them embraced.

Anything is possible, Yesenia thought. *Anything.*

Now, she looked forward to the lifetime of challenges ahead of her.

THE END

NEWSLETTER

Like this story and want to know what's coming out next, or what deals Joyce is offering on her book?

Check out Joyce's monthly newsletter at

https://joycespublishingnewsfromwideopenspaces.kit.com/a65eaa89cd

And get a free download snippet from the Martiniere Multiverse!

BOOKS AND PUBLICATIONS

The Cost of Power

Return

Snippet: Outtakes from Philip Martiniere

Crucible

Snippet: The Criminal Injustice Interview

Snippet: Sibling Warfare

Redemption

Omnibus Ebook Edition

The Martiniere Legacy

First Meetings: A Martiniere Legacy Short Story

Inheritance: The Martiniere Legacy Book One

Ascendant: The Martiniere Legacy Book Two

Realization: The Martiniere Legacy Book Three

A Belated Christmas Honeymoon: A Martiniere Legacy Short Story

The Enduring Legacy: The Martiniere Legacy Book Four

People of the Martiniere Legacy

The Heritage of Michael Martiniere: A Martiniere Legacy Novel

Broken Angel: The Lost Years of Gabriel Martiniere: A Martiniere Legacy Novel

Justine Fixes Everything: Reflections on Mortality

The Martiniere Multiverse
A Different Life: What If?
A Different Life: Now. Always. Forever.
A Very Multiversal Christmas Miracle

Goddess's Honor titles currently available (chronological order):
The Goddess's Choice: A Goddess's Honor Short Story
Beyond Honor and Other Stories: Goddess's Honor Book One
Exile's Honor: A Goddess's Honor Novelette
Birth of Sorrow: A Goddess's Honor Short Story
Pledges of Honor: Goddess's Honor Book Two
Return to Wickmasa: A Goddess's Honor Short Story
Crown Anniversary: A Goddess's Honor Short Story
Challenges of Honor: Goddess's Honor Book Three
Cleaning House: A Goddess's Honor Outtake Story
Unexpected Alliances: A Goddess's Honor Rough Draft Outtake Story
Choices of Honor: Goddess's Honor Book Four
Judgment of Honor: Goddess's Honor Book Five

Netwalk Sequence Author Preferred 2022 Editions
Life in the Shadows: Book One
Netwalk: Book Two
Netwalker Uprising: Book Three
Netwalk's Children: Book Four
Learning in Space: Book Five
Netwalking Space: Book Six

Bright Star Fair Witches
Becoming Solo: A Bright Star Fair Witches Novella

Non-Series Titles currently available:

Alien Savvy: A Western SF Novella
Klone's Stronghold
Beating the Apocalypse
Bearing Witness
Fabulist and Fantastical Worlds: A Short Story Collection
Federation Cowboy

Vella Titles:

Falcon of the Martinieres (part of *Justine Fixes Everything*)
Bearing Witness
Beating the Apocalypse
A Different Life—What If? An Alternative Martiniere Legacy Novel
Becoming Solo
A Different Life—Linda's Story: An Alternative Martiniere Legacy Novel
Federation Cowboy

Audiobooks Available:

Alien Savvy: A Western SF Novella

Released from other publishers:

"Queen of the Snows," in *Once Upon A Winter: A Folk and Fairy Tale Anthology*, edited by H. L. Macfarlane

"My Man Left Me, My Dog Hates Me, and There Goes My Truck," in *Black-Eyed Peas on New Year's Day: An Anthology of Hope*, edited by Shannon Page

"Lost Loves," in *All Worlds Wayfarer*

"The Wisdom of Robins," in *Whimsical Beasts: A Campcon Anthology*, edited by Joyce Reynolds-Ward

"The Cow at the End of the World," in *Well...It's Your Cow*, edited by Frog Jones

"To Plant or Pull Up Stakes," in *Pulling Up Stakes: A Campcon Anthology*, edited by Joyce Reynolds-Ward

"The Notice," in *Children of a Different Sky*, edited by Alma Alexander

ABOUT THE AUTHOR

The work of Joyce Reynolds-Ward includes themes of high-stakes family and political conflict, digital sentience, personal agency and control, realistic strong women, and (whenever possible) horses. She is the author of *The Netwalk Sequence* series, the *Goddess's Honor* series, *The Martiniere Legacy* series, *The People of the Martiniere Legacy* series, and the recently published *The Cost of Power* trilogy as well as standalones *Klone's Stronghold*, *Alien Savvy*, *Beating the Apocalypse*, and *Federation Cowboy*. Joyce is a Self-Published Fantasy BlogOff Semifinalist, a Writers of the Future SemiFinalist, and an Anthology Builder Finalist. She is a member of the Science Fiction and Fantasy Writers Association and a member of Soroptimists International.

www.ingramcontent.com/pod-product-compliance
Lightning Source LLC
Chambersburg PA
CBHW051232210726
48290CB00003B/918